THE MAN OF BRONZE

There is a fascination about Doc Savage, an attraction that draws men from all walks of life to his remarkable personality. And it was from this selection of manhood that Doc Savage picked his group of five remarkable aides— Ham, Monk, Renny, Long Tom and Johnny. These men lead an existence more perilous than any other group of men. For around Doc Savage there is always danger; they travel from one end of the earth to the other, righting wrongs, helping the oppressed and punishing evildoers.

Bantam Books by Kenneth Robeson
Ask your bookseller for the books you have missed

TUNNEL TERROR

A Doc Savage® Adventure
Kenneth Robeson

TUNNEL TERROR
A Bantam Book / published by arrangement with
The Condé Nast Publications Inc.

PRINTING HISTORY
Originally published in DOC SAVAGE Magazine August 1940
Bantam edition / February 1979

ISBN 0–553–11191–4

Published simultaneously in the United States and Canada

PRINTED IN THE UNITED STATES OF AMERICA

Contents

Chapter I

STRANGE FOG

Hardrock Hennesey had once been called the toughest little mucker who had ever crawled through a river's belly. It was said that if a drill broke while he was on a tunnel job, he could eat his way through rock. He looked as though he had been eating rock now.

He spat on the dusty highway, stared up and down the deserted stretch of dark road, and started swearing. He swore for three minutes. He was just getting warmed up. And then he shrugged disgustedly, spat again.

He murmured, "Ah, nuts!" and started hiking along the dusty road once again. He wished to the blasted devil that he had never left New York City.

But there were no tunnels being constructed at the moment in New York, and here—in the West—they were calling for miners and muckers on the greatest water tunnel ever built. A tunnel that was going to convey nine hundred million gallons of water a day a hundred miles into a great city.

And Hardrock Hennesey needed a job. He was broke. Like every mucker or miner who had ever helped build a tunnel, he was broke between jobs. Money came fast in this game. And it was spent the same way. It was a wild, reckless—and dangerous—existence.

Thus he was bumming his way through the country. According to estimations, he had only about three more miles to go. But on this out-of-the-way back highway, a car hadn't passed him in the last hour.

It was some time after nine o'clock, and the moon

was just coming up when the farmer came rattling along in his old flivver.

Hardrock Hennesey spun around. His leathery, flint-hard features brightened. That is, a few more wrinkles appeared on his scarred, old-looking face. He hitched up his trousers around his skinny waist and got his thumb stuck out in a "how-about-a-ride" gesture.

The farmer rolled his heap right on past Hardrock Hennesey.

Hardrock swore. This time he wasn't very subtle about it. He jumped up and down and kicked at the dust with his worn shoes. He just wished he had his hands on that blankety-blank so-and-so's throat. He wished—

Ahead, beyond a slight dip in the road, there floated back the sound of worn brake shoes chattering. The flivver was stopping! The farmer must have decided, after looking Hardrock over as he passed, that it was all right to give him a lift.

Hardrock went into a sprint, his thin, hard-as-nails legs carrying his tough little body along furiously. He arrived at the dip in the road, started to yell, "Hey—"

He skidded to a stop in the dust and stared.

He gawked at sight of what might have been ground mist ahead. The night was warm enough, and this part of the road in a hollow cool enough to cause slight ground fog.

And yet what he saw wasn't fog. He could see through it. It was like the kind of mirage effect you see coming off tarred pavements on August days. It wasn't quite white, nor quite gray, and it seemed to float and swirl up from the dust.

Yet it wasn't this that held Hardrock Hennesey spellbound. He rubbed his eyes, deciding that he'd never drink any more of that stuff that he'd bought last night. It must have been distilled from coal. Perhaps he was getting astigmatism.

Because he stared at the fog ahead—the stuff that he was positive he could see through—and he couldn't see what should be parked there. No car. No farmer.

Hardrock Hennesey growled, "Say, who's kiddin' who?" and stalked ahead toward the vague stuff that was like mist. He reached the spot.

And he let out a whoop of pain and leaped backward as though someone had hit him with a ten-foot pole. He jerked up and down, waving his hands and blowing on his fingers. He felt of his face, drew his hands away quickly.

It was just as though he had been burned by live steam!

The tough little tunnel worker backed off from the spot, squinting out of his intense gray eyes. He got down on his hands and knees in the dust. He stared. He tried to see beneath the peculiar, wispy-gray stuff ahead. In a way, it made him think of a huge spider's web.

He got up again, walked cautiously forward and stuck out a questing finger.

The finger felt as though he'd plunged it into the spout of a hot teakettle.

"What the hell?" Hardrock Hennesey asked himself, and started doing some more enthusiastic swearing.

He knew damned right well he wasn't drunk. He hadn't had a drink all day. And he didn't have a hangover.

He moved to the side of the road, climbed a fence that adjoined a farmer's field, started circling the funny gray stuff that floated in the air in the dip in the road.

Hardrock Hennesey was certain he could see through the stuff. And he knew, absolutely, that he'd heard the old flivver come to a chattering stop. But where was it now? Where was the farmer?

Dammit, something was cockeyed here and he was quite sure it wasn't himself. He edged toward the foggy stuff.

And got burned again. Howling with pain, Hardrock Hennesey once more backed off and sat down on a rock to watch the stuff. He rubbed his eyes. He stared at his raw-red fingertips. He couldn't figure it out.

He sat there for perhaps fifteen minutes, and no other cars came along, and the night was very quiet, with the moon climbing up in the sky like a white, round face.

Hardrock Hennesey had once whipped a dozen muckers in a tunnel riot. For a small-looking man— who, from his weathered features, could have been forty or sixty—he was about the hardest individual on two feet. Nothing much ever scared him.

But there was something uncanny about this strange fog stuff that had stopped him now. He put his head in his gnarled hands and sat there thinking, and he wondered if he was cracking up. Perhaps too many years of working "under pressure" had caught up with him. Maybe.

He looked up, and the fog had dispersed.

Hardrock jumped up, started carefully forward, stretching out his hands in front of him. This time they didn't touch anything hot. There seemed to be nothing ahead.

Nothing, that is, except the farmer's old car. He saw it clearly now, there in the roadway. He gulped. He stood very still and rubbed his eyes and swore. His fists knotted, and he stalked furiously forward. Somebody was damned well going to pay for pulling this gag on him. And that somebody was going to be that gangling farmer, that guy seated behind the wheel.

But there was no gag about the dead man slumped over the steering wheel of the car. Hardrock Hennesey jerked back in horror at sight of the withered features, and skin that was like old, brown leather. He stared at the man.

The corpse that was like a dried-up mummy!

Hardrock Hennesey had, at various times in his dangerous career, seen men die. He had observed half a dozen men buried—smothered beneath muck in a

.tunnel cave-in; he had seen a giant Negro shot through planking and sand and water in a "blow" beneath the East River. He had seen men crushed to death beneath tons of falling rock.

But what he observed now sort of sickened him. He took off his dusty old hat and wiped at his perspiring brow. Then he reached out an inquiring finger and touched the corpse's face.

The browned, dried skin literally cracked beneath his touch. The entire face was shrunken like something out of a tomb thousands of years old.

Hardrock Hennesey shuddered. But he got up nerve enough to reach inside the car and push the mummified thing across the seat. Then he climbed in behind the wheel and started up the engine.

He had to get to the town that he knew was ahead; he had to tell them of what he had seen. He figured he might have to bust a few noses before he got anyone to believe his story.

The car ran forward perhaps a quarter of a mile before it started hammering and bucking. Hardrock Hennesey could even *smell* the engine heat. Then the motor stopped completely, "froze up."

Hardrock climbed out, looked into the radiator. He stuck his finger in the top. Dry! He raised the hood and tried the petcock drain located at the bottom of the radiator. No water ran out.

Puzzled, Hardrock recalled that the car had been running all right when it passed him on the road the first time. Even though it had rattled considerably, there had been no indication of its being without water.

He noted the license number of the old car, went back to take one look at the mummified farmer. He'd have to walk the remainder of the way into town.

He was standing up on the running board, and just as he started to turn away again something that was on the back seat caught his eye.

It was a package, neatly wrapped and apparently addressed for mailing. Hardrock leaned over and looked at the thing. He picked it up.

The package was about six inches square and half
an inch thick. It was very light in weight. It was
addressed merely:

To:
> Clark Savage, Jr.
> New York City
> New York

Hardrock Hennesey stared.

"Hell's fire!" he exploded, and got down off the
car and started running down the road toward town.
He had heard of Clark Savage, Jr. In fact, he knew a
fellow who worked for him. What connection had this
mummy with the remarkable person known as Doc
Savage?

A mile down the road Hardrock came to a roadside tavern from which was coming enough racket to
tell him a certain fact. The racket from inside indicated either a revival meeting or a riot. Ten chances to
one, it was the latter. Also, it was Saturday night.

And that meant—tunnel muckers!

Hardrock Hennesey hurried inside and immediately big men lined up at the bar turned and hailed
him and started yelling things like:

"Well, you old buzzard!"

"Hardrock! Line up, boy, and drink!"

"Say, boy!" another man yelled. "It's about time
Hardrock showed up. Now you'll see some *work* on
this new tunnel job!"

A new man among the muckers asked a question
of an old-timer. He was told:

"Look, fella, Hardrock Hennesey's the greatest
little mucker that ever ate hardrock. He ain't afraid of
hell and dynamite. He's worked on every big job from
New York to Frisco, the South, everywhere."

Tunnel workers—miners and muckers and hardrock men—probably make up the greatest fraternity
of workmen in the world. You'll find the same gangs
on jobs from Boston to Alaska. You'll find them working like demons, drinking hard and fighting on their

nights off. And you'll find them sticking together. Hardrock Hennesey was perhaps the best hardrock man in the game. He was known everywhere.

Hands now slapped him on the back and drinks were pushed in his face.

But suddenly, and strangely, other muckers realized that their old friend was not accepting the drinks or returning their greetings. He was just standing there staring at them oddly, his intense gray eyes wide and bright.

"Look," Hardrock demanded. "I'm not drunk, am I? And—"

Someone laughed. "Hell, no! Maybe that's what's wrong with you. Come on, fella, catch up!"

"And I don't look crazy, do I?" Hardrock Hennesey managed to get in.

The men quieted somewhat. They grouped around the hard little tunnel worker and looked at him puzzledly.

Someone in the group finally managed to describe the thing that everyone saw—but was afraid to admit.

"I'll be damned!" the man exclaimed. "Look at 'im! Hardrock is . . . well, he's *scared!*"

Just about that moment someone got a drink into Hardrock's hand. It was a water glass half full of whiskey, a hundred proof. Hardrock Hennesey took the stuff down at a gulp.

He grabbed the one who had called him scared. His right fist traveled in a short arc. The fellow went down without even a grunt.

Then Hardrock rapped, "Now, listen to this."

He started talking. He told about walking along the road a mile or so back. He mentioned the peculiar fog, the misty stuff that you ought to be able to see through—but somehow could not.

He said, "The stuff burned me!"

Someone asked, "You mean . . . the fog?"

"Whatever was there around the car that I couldn't see," Hardrock said.

Men stared. Someone laughed.

Hardrock grabbed the big man and slapped his face, and the fellow's head jerked around on his neck.

"You ever see a man change into a mummy?" Hardrock demanded.

Apparently no one had ever seen such a phenomenon. Hardrock led the way toward the door.

"You guys come along with me," he ordered, "an' I'll show you something that'll knock your ears down."

He led the men back along the dusty roadway. There were perhaps two dozen tunnel workers in all. Big men. Hard men. Guys who knew Hardrock Hennesey from former jobs. They were now convinced that hard-boiled little Hardrock Hennesey was far from being drunk or crazy.

They were all now anxious to see a farmer who had become a mummy. They pushed past one another as they arrived at the old battered car.

They stared. They turned and looked at tough Hardrock Hennesey and their faces were grim.

A worker said, "This ain't a very funny gag."

"Let's take him apart!" suggested another.

But Hardrock elbowed them aside and himself moved up to the car.

The mummified man had disappeared.

This wasn't the only thing that held him rigid. His gaze had jerked to the rear seat, to the object that he had left there. It was the one thing that might have explained a part of this mystery. Hardrock was thinking of the small package that had been addressed to the man known as Doc Savage.

The package, also, was missing.

Chapter II

CALL FOR HELP

The free-for-all battle that followed was somewhat of a honey.

It started when the fellow who was new to the

gang called Hardrock Hennesey a liar. Hardrock climbed down off the old car's running board and commenced throwing punches in various directions.

Several of the muckers had had enough to drink to get sore about the whole business. They joined the melee enthusiastically.

Hardrock Hennesey knocked two men down, swung on a third and growled, "*Now* are you convinced, wise guy? I tell you the fog burned me. It musta burned up that farmer in the car!"

"Crazy as a loon!" said the big tunnel worker, and that got him a bust on the nose. He howled with pain and sailed into tough Hardrock Hennesey. Others helped out. They finally got Hardrock down in the dusty road and tried to pound some sense into his head.

But the more they pounded, the more Hardrock Hennesey swore and kicked and battered away at his opponents.

By the time several State troopers arrived in their white-painted car, the battle was really going great guns. And it was fifteen minutes before Hardrock was finally subdued and carried off toward the local jail.

That was after Hardrock Hennesey had tried to tell some of the troopers his story. For now that they had enjoyed a good fight, few of the tunnel workers wished to see their old friend carted off to the local hoosegow. And so they merely suggested that Hardrock Hennesey repeat what he had told them about the mysterious fog and a farmer who became a mummy.

Hardrock was halfway through his account when one trooper looked at another. Then they grabbed Hardrock and piled him in their car.

"Balmy!" was their opinion.

From conversation that Hardrock Hennesey heard as they rode toward town, he gathered that the troopers had recognized the old flivver. It appeared the farmer's name was Brown—Zeke Brown.

As one officer remarked, "Zeke's so damn' tight he's always running out of gas. He must have run out again and walked to the village."

"That's about it," a second trooper agreed.

Hardrock Hennesey started to put in, "Listen, he didn't walk *nowheres*. He's dead, I tell you! He's as dead as—"

"Shuddup!" a trooper rapped, and slapped him on the mouth.

Hardrock subsided again. And shortly the trooper car drew up before a small building that bordered the town ahead. In the distance, Hardrock Hennesey could see a towering steel framework, some buildings and the reflection of floodlights against the night sky. That would be Shaft 9, where he had been headed. Shaft 9, one of the many units in the tunnel project.

The troopers climbed out, stood aside, motioned Hardrock Hennesey out also.

Hardrock came out of the car in a flying leap, bowled over two of the three officers, clipped the third on the jaw, circled the small jail, and took flight in the woods that pressed up close behind the building.

Angry bees arrived over his head. The bees were bullets, and they were from the troopers' guns. They thunked into trees, and were too close for comfort. Luckily, Hardrock Hennesey got deep into the woods, and none of the slugs found him.

He kept running. He ran for perhaps a mile before he paused to listen. The moon was overhead now, and it gave enough light to help him find his way. There was no sound behind him save the occasional scurrying of some small animal through the brush.

Hardrock made his way back toward the highway again. A half hour later, cautiously, he emerged on the roadway and stared up and down. He was at a point beyond the town, and in the distance he could see the light of Shaft 9.

The old fellow seated on the rock beside the road watched Hardrock Hennesey's cautious movements. Then he asked:

"Reckon you saw it too, eh?"

Hardrock jumped. He had not seen the old man. He gawked at him now.

The fellow was all of ninety years old. He was

bent over and withered. He leaned on a cane that he must have cut out of a gnarled piece of hickory. His withered old skin looked like that of a—

A mummy!

The thought gave Hardrock Hennesey a start.

But then this mummy was alive. What was it he had said?

"See *what?*" Hardrock demanded suspiciously. He looked up and down the road, but he saw no one approaching.

"The thing that follows you in the night," said the old man. He sounded worried.

"What thing?"

Something about the tone of the old fellow's voice made a chill slide down Hardrock Hennesey's spine.

"The thing that is like a ghost. I reckon, mister, I've seen it a dozen times. It almost got me tother night. Reckon it'll get me any time now, too. I'm too old to get away from it."

Hardrock swallowed. Maybe this old geezer was nuts. And yet he remembered the strange thing that had happened to himself. Thinking of that, he recalled the package.

The package that had been addressed to Doc Savage, and which had disappeared.

He suddenly grabbed the old fellow's arm and asked, "Maybe you can tell me where I can find a phone." And, as an afterthought, "A phone where maybe there won't be too many people around listening when I make a call?"

The oldster nodded. He almost creaked when he moved, pointing toward town.

"You foller this road a piece until you come to Sam's garage, and in there you'll find a phone, mister. Sam'll probably be across the road at his house. He only comes over when someone honks for gas. But you go right ahead and use the phone, and he won't mind a bit."

"Thanks," said Hardrock quickly, and got away from there. The old fellow had sort of got under his skin, what with all that had happened to him in the past hour.

He reached the garage without being spotted by any troopers with guns, without being seen by anyone.

A light was turned on above the single gas pump outside the place. As the old man had said, Sam was apparently across the road in his house. There were lights visible in the kitchen of the place.

So much the better, Hardrock Hennesey figured. He preferred that no one know of the phone call he was going to make.

Two minutes later, using the phone he located inside the garage building, he was connected with the New York headquarters of Doc Savage. Hardrock made a single request. He would like to speak to a man named Colonel John Renwick, the engineer in the organization of Doc Savage.

He got a break. Colonel John Renwick happened, at that moment, to be at the headquarters.

A great, booming voice came over the wire. Hardrock yanked the receiver away from his ear. It had been so long since he had seen his old friend that he had forgotten about the giant-sized fellow's bull-like voice.

"Yes?" said the man on the other end.

"This you, Renny?" Hardrock asked.

"Yes. Who's this?" the crashing voice demanded.

Hardrock gave details about himself. He finished with, "Remember that Hudson River tunnel job where they called you in for advice? Remember that fight one day up in the heading?"

The man named Renny suddenly laughed. Hardrock thought the receiver diaphragm would split.

"Hardrock, you old buzzard!" Renny said. "How's everything? Where are you?"

Apparently the fellow named Renny was glad to hear from his old friend.

Hardrock Hennesey said tensely, "You, Renny, you gotta come here."

"Where?"

Hardrock outlined the particular section of mountainous country where he was. He mentioned Yellow River Dam, a mammoth storage shed that was being constructed in conjunction with the one-hundred-mile-long tunnel project. Yellow River Dam was only a few miles above Shaft 9, where Hardrock hoped to get a job.

"There's something funny up here," Hardrock continued.

"What do you mean?"

"Well," said Hardrock Hennesey worriedly, "there was a fella with a package for Doc Savage. He died. He died, and he looked like a mummy."

The man named Renny said, "Hardrock, you've been drinking again!"

The hard-boiled little tunnel worker rapped, "Listen, Renny; this isn't any joke. An' I'm cold sober. You just listen to this. There was a peculiar sort of fog. It was sort of transparent stuff, and again it wasn't. Well, this farmer—this fella that died—got into the stuff and I couldn't get near him. He's the one who had the package for Doc Savage."

"Have you the package now?"

"No, it's gone. But about this fog—"

"Yes?"

Hardrock paused, wiping at his brow with the crook of his arm. He realized that it was a warm night, but suddenly he felt unusually hot.

He continued: "This fog stuff was as hot as a furnace. It burned like live steam. Later, I found this farmer and he looked just like a dried-up mummy!"

Renny said nothing for a moment. Then he put in, "And he's the one who had the package for Doc Savage?"

"Yes. And, Renny, there's something else!"

"What?"

"It's—"

This time, Hardrock Hennesey *felt* the heat that seemed to crawl over him like something alive and menacing. He turned slightly away from the phone, staring over his shoulder.

And he let out a yell as the instrument slipped from his stiff fingers.

Because the fog stuff was right there behind him, floating like tendrils of clawing, ghostlike fingers through the open doorway. Hardrock Hennesey could apparently see through the strange stuff, and yet couldn't. It was uncanny.

He leaped out of the chair where he had been seated, stared frantically around the small space. His face already felt as if it was frying in the steamy heat. The stuff was slowly enveloping him with ethereal, opaque fingers.

With a gasp of horror, Hardrock Hennesey jumped toward the rear of the room. He sought a window. But before he could locate one, the floating, peculiar fog was upon him. He sank down in a shuddering heap, and as the strange veil dropped over him he let out a frantic yell.

"Renny! Help! *It's got me!*"

Chapter III

LIVING DEAD MAN

The fast, streamlined plane came down out of the night sky, circled the field, landed and taxied to a stop not far from the roadside gas station in the mountains.

The first person who stepped out of the plane was indeed a strange-looking individual. He was about as broad as he was wide. All parts of his exposed body contained bristly, red hair that looked like stubby, thin nails. He had incredibly homely features made to hold up traffic at street corners.

In a squeaky, almost childlike voice he piped, "Blazes! We oughta fumigate that plane. Something's been bitin' me all the way from New York."

Without bending forward, the homely one scratched at his leg, in the vicinity of his knee. This was accomplished because the man's arms dangled well below his knees. He was built like an oversized ape.

From the plane had followed a slender, nattily dressed man with a waspish waist. He carried a neat black cane. He frowned in disgust at the apelike individual and said, "Did you ever try soap and water for that?"

Immediately, the hairy one made a roundhouse swing at the dapper-looking man. He glared and said, "That sounded like a dirty remark."

The slender one grinned. "It was suited to the occasion, you hairy baboon!"

Just then, two queer-looking animals scurried from the plane door. One was a pig, a scrawny-looking pig with beanpole legs and a snout made for rummaging inside long tin cans. The other animal was a runt-sized ape that looked suspiciously like the hairy individual who spoke in the childlike voice.

The runt ape moved toward the person who looked not unlike himself, and took a nip out of the man's leg. The spot where the animal took the bite was right where the fellow had been scratching.

Abruptly, understanding leaped into the hairy one's eyes.

"Ye-o-ow!" he squalled. "It's that blasted Chemistry that's been biting me all the way up from New York!"

He made a dive for the chimp. The tall, well-dressed man got in the way and quickly swung the animal up in his arms. Apparently Chemistry was his pet.

He kicked at the scrawny pig, remarked icily, "Take that Habeas away from here before I annihilate him! He must have fleas!"

There threatened to be a riot between the two men until the giant-sized figure stepped out of the plane and said, "We seem to be missing something." He pointed to the gas-station building down the field.

The third arrival was the man whom Hardrock Hennesey had phoned—Colonel John Renwick, but better known as Renny to his friends and the other aids in Doc Savage's organization. Renny was six inches over six feet, weighed well over two hundred pounds, and had hands like quart-size pails. He also had a gloomy-looking face which reminded you of an under-taker without clients.

When he spoke, his booming voice shattered the summer night's quietude.

It was the hairy fellow who demanded, "Missing what? Where?" He squinted out of his small eyes ·to-ward the spot that Renny had indicated.

"There seems to be some sort of fight in progress," Renny explained. He turned to the well-dressed man who had been ready to clout the apish fellow. "See it, Ham?"

"Ham," apparently, did. His face brightened. He set down the pet chimp.

"Monk must be slipping," he remarked coolly. "First time he's ever passed up a fight in his life!"

Obviously Monk was the hairy individual with whom he'd been arguing.

Monk let out a howl as he spotted some sort of mix-up taking place over near the gas station. His short legs took him in a wild gallop across the field.

Renny and the one called Ham followed along in time to enter into a shambles that sounded like a dog fight with a stray alley cat cornered in the middle.

But it was hairy Monk who was in the center of the fight. Around him fists swung and there were as-sorted kinds of cursing.

The faces of the fellows behind the swinging fists looked like something made to frighten small children. They were of the thug variety.

A rotund, red-faced man was on the outside of the melee, jumping up and down and yelling.

"These men just broke into my gas station!" he screamed. "Help!"

Giant Renny plowed into the group and his fists started swinging. Men were knocked sprawling. The sound the giant engineer's fists made as they hit various individuals was like the noise a chunk of cement makes striking soft leather.

Renny looked unusually gloomy—whereas he was probably enjoying himself immensely.

As was the one named Ham. Instead of using

rough-house tactics, he merely flicked at some of the battling men with what appeared to be a slender sword. He had drawn the sword from the black cane, which was obviously some sort of sheath.

Two men sighed and lay down and seemed to forget all about the fight. They could hardly know that the end of the sword cane contained a mild anaesthetic drug that would hold them unconscious for some time.

Three fellows broke loose of the surging battle and took out for the nearby woods.

It was hairy Monk who howled, "What the blazes! I was doin' fine all by myself. What's the idea of interrupting?"

He glared at well-dressed Ham. Someone cracked Monk in the jaw during this momentary intermission. Monk howled, grabbed the one who had hit him, upended him and started bouncing the fellow's head on the ground.

And all the time the plump gas-station owner hopped up and down outside the fighting mass and yelled things like, "Help! Murder! Police!"

The police arrived in the form of a State-trooper car loaded with husky, powerful young men in snappy uniforms. But before they could swing into the battle, three more men had ducked clear and disappeared into the nearby woods.

All those that were left lay sprawled in the dusty roadway. That is, all except hairy Monk, smooth-looking Ham—whose collar was not even disturbed—and giant Renny.

Monk complained, "Blast it! An' we was just gettin' started!"

A trooper rapped, "What goes on?"

The red-faced station owner, now that the law had arrived in force, stepped forward and said, "There were half a dozen tunnel workers passing. I had just discovered the crooks who broke into my station. I yelled for help, and the tunnel men were helping me out."

He turned, indicated the three who had arrived

from the plane. "I don't know about these three. I don't know whether they were helping these tunnel men or the crooks!"

It appeared that all six men lying on the ground were tunnel workers. One at a time, they started sitting up and rubbing at bruised jaws.

The thugs—the ones who had broken into the station—had disappeared to parts unknown.

It was quick-thinking Ham who asked, "Why did they break into your station, mister?"

The fat owner apparently didn't know.

"The fight," he said, "started before I could investigate."

The troopers were looking at Ham and his partners suspiciously. Ham said, "Perhaps we should explain." He looked at big Renny, and the engineer nodded.

"Explain what?" one trooper asked.

"About Hardrock Hennesey."

There were seven State troopers. All stiffened at Ham's words. Because all knew of the crazy story that had been told by Hardrock Hennesey earlier tonight, a cockeyed yarn about a mummified man and a fog that burned.

"What do you know about Hardrock Hennesey?" one of the troopers demanded.

"This," put in Renny. "He called me in New York. He told us about some sort of mystery taking place up here. Since he's an old friend, we hopped up here to investigate. And we ran into this."

Renny made no mention of Doc Savage. He did not explain that Ham was really Brigadier General Theodore Marley Brooks, a well-known graduate of the Harvard Law School, and the attorney in the organization of Doc Savage.

Or that Monk, the hairy individual, was really Lieutenant Colonel Andrew Blodgett Mayfair, a renowned chemist—regardless of his resemblance to a belligerent gorilla.

The two pets, Habeas and Chemistry, had scurried back to the plane.

The troopers, their forces augmented, were still

seeking tough little Hardrock Hennesey. Naturally they were somewhat suspicious of Renny and his partners.

"Where's Hardrock Hennesey now?" one inquired.

Monk stuck out his jaw. "Brother," he piped, "that's what we come up here to find out. Hardrock was talkin' to Renny, an' all of a sudden he cut short his call and started yellin' for help. Something's phony as hell around here."

One trooper stared curiously at Monk's ugly features and commented, "Yes, I guess so."

Monk was ready to take a poke at the fellow when Ham suggested quickly, "It might be a good idea to look around. There must have been a reason for crooks breaking into this man's gas station. We had Hardrock Hennesey's call traced—and it came from here."

Everyone shoved inside the small building, and it was in there that they found the mummified corpse.

The thing that had once been a man was quite hideous.

The whole body had shrunken, as though drained of every bit of moisture that had ever been in it. Skin hung onto the skeleton that was left like dried-up, dirty, stiff cloth. The features of the face had shrunken so that it was imposssible to tell whether the man had been young—or very old.

One of the tunnel men had pushed forward. A little while ago he had been pretty drunk; now he was sober.

He murmured in awe, "It . . . it's Hardrock!"

Another mucker agreed. "Yep. Look at his clothes. That's what Hardrock Hennesey was wearing when we saw him tonight."

The speaker's voice grew hushed. "And we didn't believe Hardrock when he tried to tell us about that farmer!"

A trooper had been going through the mummified man's clothing. He removed a letter from an inside pocket, opened it, read something.

Then he nodded. "It's Hardrock Hennesey, all right. This is a letter of introduction to the super at Shaft 9."

Everyone started talking at once. During this, Renny stepped up to one of the troopers and requested, "Mind if I just look at him a moment? He was an old friend." Renny indicated the shrunken corpse on the floor.

The trooper shrugged. "O. K. by me, fella."

Renny stooped down while Monk and Ham were busy questioning the tunnel men. No one could explain the mystery. But for big men who pitted themselves against constant dangers below the earth's surface, who were in the habit of treating life as something that might be snuffed out at any time, they now looked awed.

One said, "I wonder what Hardrock meant about that fog."

"What fog?" asked a trooper who, apparently, had not heard Hardrock Hennesey's story earlier.

Before anyone could answer, there was a shout of excitement from outside the small building. Monk and Ham were first outside.

The stout man, Sam, who owned the station, was indicating a large barrel that was on a small platform beside the building.

"Look!" he cried. "It's completely dry!"

Monk squinted inside the barrel, and then at the fat man.

"So what?" he wanted to know.

"Listen," the stout man went on, "that barrel was almost plumb full of water a couple of hours ago. It's a rain barrel."

"Maybe somebody dumped it," Monk said.

But the man shook his head. "How could they?" he demanded. "It's fastened down!"

No one had an answer for that.

It was Monk who ambled inside, took another look at the mummified man, then came outside again and stood staring at the empty rain barrel. But, for once, he kept his mouth shut. Ham gave him a peculiar regard.

While fat Sam was trying to figure what had become of his rain water, Renny drew his two partners aside and murmured. "There's something we ought to investigate." The powerful engineer had a time trying to keep his voice down to a whisper.

"Investigate what?" Ham queried.

"Hardrock Hennesey."

"But he's dead!" the dapper lawyer insisted.

"Come on," suggested Renny, and he led the way as they slipped away from the group. He said nothing until they had returned to their plane. There, Renny locked the cabin door.

The pets, who had been chasing each other wildly around the field, joined them.

Monk, puzzled, demanded, "What are you gonna do, Renny?"

"Find Hardrock Hennesey," the big engineer said.

Monk pointed back toward the gas station. "You mean that—"

Renny nodded.

He said, "You see, Hardrock, for a tough little guy, was always somewhat superstitious. He always carried a miniature rabbit's foot on a chain around his neck. But the rabbit's foot was not being worn by that fellow who became a mummy."

Ham had an answer for that.

Someone could have removed it," he said.

"Naturally," agreed Renny. "But they couldn't have removed the thing that was on Hardrock's chest. I recall it very well."

"What?"

"Hardrock always figured that some day he might die in a river tunnel. In water. So he once had a mermaid tattooed on his chest. He was a great one for doing crazy things like that."

"And there is no mermaid tattooed on the man's chest back there?" Ham asked.

"Correct."

Monk's small eyes brightened. "Then Hardrock must still be alive!"

Ham gave his homely partner a sour look.

"Sometimes," the lawyer said icily, "you almost show signs of intelligence!"

It looked, for the moment, as if there was going to be a fight. For these two unusual fellows liked nothing better than an argument.

But Renny stopped it with the remark, "The logical place to start would be at Shaft 9, near here. That's where Hardrock was headed in the first place. We'll walk."

They started out, hairy Monk commenting in his squeaky voice, "I'm gonna enjoy meetin' that Hardrock Hennesey. Bet he's a great fighter, from what I've heard."

Ham said, "You've got a one-track mind, you hairy mistake. What we really would like to learn is what was in that package Hardrock mentioned. The package addressed to Doc."

Monk growled something.

"I'm still more interested in that little tunnel mucker," he insisted.

The hairy chemist was due for a surprise when they got to Shaft 9. But before that happened, they ran into something else.

It was the excited, shoving, noisy argument that was taking place near the opening of the shaft.

Chapter IV

THE DISAPPEARING MEN

Shaft 9 was only one in the series of openings that formed a chain in the great water-tunnel project. South of here there were others; just north, a great dam that was nearing completion. The dam would be used as a storage shed for excess water that came down out of the mountains.

Aboveground there were various buildings. There

was a powerhouse. Another smaller building housed the machinery for running the shaft lift that plunged more than fifteen hundred feet into the earth. Above all was the constant throbbing of a unit that drove fresh air down to the workmen far below. A pipe that carried this air led to the shaft itself and crawled down its sides. It looked like a fat, black snake.

Overhead were bright floodlights. The shaft was using three shifts of miners and muckers. The pile of rock that had been carried up out of the new tunnel looked like a small mountain beyond the shaft buildings.

It was at the shaft opening that the trouble was taking place.

Monk, Ham and Renny moved close. The pets remained at a safe distance.

Monk grinned. His eyes brightened hopefully. "Let's join the fight," he suggested.

"Let Renny handle this, dunce!" Ham rapped coolly.

While they waited, big Renny moved forward and talked to some of the grimy workmen on the edges of the group. He returned shortly.

"There's been some kind of queer accident down in the tunnel," he announced. "Some of these fellows want to quit. Others are trying to keep them on the job. There's liable to be trouble."

"What happened down there?" Monk demanded.

"From what I gathered," Renny said, "a man was found dead. Others are saying they saw a queer fog. They're afraid to go back to work. There seems to be some sort of jinx on the place."

Ham said, "Let's talk to them and explain that Hardrock Hennesey is not dead—as far as we know."

As they moved up to the group of arguing and struggling workmen, Renny and Ham took it for granted that Monk was right behind them.

He wasn't.

Monk saw the thin, quick-moving man in overalls, a fellow who was acting suspiciously. The man had come out of the surrounding darkness and stepped hesitatingly toward the packed circle of arguing tunnel workers. For just a moment, light from one of the floodlamps illuminated his leathery, oldish features. It revealed the open flannel shirt at the throat.

In that brief instant when Monk turned, the strange-acting man was quite close to him. And so the hairy chemist saw the thing on the man's chest when it was exposed, momentarily, to the light.

A tatooed mermaid, as large as your hat!

Instantly the fellow had swung back and disappeared in the shadows. With Monk taking out behind him!

The trail led wide of the shaft buildings and several huge Mack trucks parked nearby. It led beyond the small mountain that was broken-up rock taken from the tunnel bore.

Monk saw the wiry little guy disappear toward a square, steel building set well apart from any others. A big red sign on the side of the building warned:

DYNAMITE

Monk ducked behind a truck in order to watch. In doing so, he momentarily lost track of the fellow he was trailing. He waited several moments, not certain whether his quarry had gone into the dynamite storage shack or not.

Hairy Monk was not one to wait long on anything. He came out from behind the truck and hurried up to the small building. He saw that the door was ajar.

Damned funny, he thought, that the guy was coming *here.* And that Hardrock Hennesey should be that strange-acting fellow! Hardrock Hennesey, with a mermaid tattooed on his chest!

Monk slammed into the building.

And a small hard fist slammed into his face, while another got hold of his stubby, bristly hair.

The girl's voice snapped out, "Brother, you sure got one hell of a nerve!"

Monk stared.

The girl had been standing to one side of the

door, just inside the building. There was a dim light glowing, and now it revealed her quite plainly.

Abruptly, the girl was staring with as much open-mouthed amazement as was the homely-faced chemist.

The girl said, "Maybe I should scream!" as she looked at Monk.

Then Monk grinned. He grinned because he liked what he saw, because the chemist had a fondness for the ladies—especially pretty ones—and this girl here had features and a shape that contained just about everything.

Her slender, boyish form was startlingly outlined by the whipcord breeches that she wore. Her flannel shirt, open at the throat, emphasized the lovely curve of her throat.

She had fine, smooth features, and Monk thought that her eyes were aquamarine.

She also had red hair. And a temper.

She took an angry step toward the hairy chemist and rapped, "What are you staring it?"

Monk grinned. Strangely the chemist always went over big with the ladies. Perhaps it was because of his utterly homely face and nerve.

He said, "Put you in a silk dress and a picture hat, and you'd have Dietrich backed off the boards."

The girl's trim, taut figure relaxed a bit. There was no woman that could hear that kind of flattery without reacting to it.

She asked, "Just who *are* you?"

Monk liked the way she held her chin and the manner in which her hands were clenched at her sides. He was willing to bet she could well handle herself.

"I was lookin' for a fella named Hardrock Hennesey," he said. "Thought I saw him come in here. I was gonna—"

The girl gasped. "Hardrock? You . . . you've seen *him?*"

"If he's a bird with a tattooed mermaid on his chest—yes," offered Monk.

Suddenly the girl's firm hand was gripping his powerful arm. Her green eyes were bright with worry.

"Then you've got to help me," she blurted. "You've got to help me locate Hardrock. He can help us. I've been trying to find him."

"You know him, lady?"

"Of course. For years. He's the only one that can explain."

"Explain what?"

Caution came into the girl's eyes.

"You haven't yet answered my question," she reminded. "Just who are you?"

"Ever hear of a man named Doc Savage?" the chemist asked.

The girl's eyes narrowed; she seemed to give a slight start. She said carefully, "Yes, I have. Why?"

"Well," Monk went on, "Hardrock Hennesey found something that was addressed to Doc Savage from a man up here. A guy who got killed strangely. That's why I want to find Hardrock Hennesey."

Monk then went on to explain how he was the chemist in Doc Savage's organization. His chest swelled a little, as he added: "There are a few men in the world who consider themselves greater chemists—but that's only because of professional jealously. I'm broad-minded enough to overlook—"

Beside them, from outside the doorway, Ham's cutting voice said, "Only reason this baboon is broad-minded is because he was dropped out of a tree when he was very young. On his head. You'll note that it is almost flat—"

Monk let out a roar and swung on his nattily attired partner.

"Listen, shyster—" he started.

But Ham was smiling gallantly at the red-haired girl. He introduced himself. He pushed between Monk and the girl, then used his most effective manner.

As a famous Harvard Law School graduate, Ham was an orator when it came to talking. It was also his ambition to take any girl away from hairy Monk.

He was saying now, "Perhaps I can help you, my dear girl. You see, I am an accomplished—"

"—father!" Monk added. "He's got thirteen funny-faced kids, all kept locked up in the Bellevue psychopathic ward!"

Ham swung on the chemist. The two pets, Habeas and the runt ape, appeared behind them. They started glaring at one another like their masters. For Monk's favorite gag was to tell pretty young girls that his partner had thirteen children, whereas Ham was a bachelor.

It was the girl who stopped the argument. She moved between the two, knotted her fists, said coolly, "Are you two going to stop acting like boys, or do I have to slap one of you down?"

She sounded as though she could really do it.

Monk gulped. Ham stared. For such a lovely-faced girl, there was something about her attitude that said she had spent much time around construction workers—and could handle herself.

Both Ham and Monk grinned sheepishly.

"Guess we better start lookin' for Hardrock Hennesey," suggested hairy Monk.

The girl nodded. "That's better. And now, if you say you saw him, there's one place to start."

She had locked the shed door behind them; they were returning toward the spot where tunnel workers had been staging a near riot.

"Where?" Ham wanted to know.

"The shaft. That Hardrock will want to see some of his old pals, if he *is* here. He'll be down there in the tunnel, first chance he gets. Try to keep *him* out!"

The two Doc Savage aids learned that the girl's name was Chick Lancaster. It appeared her brother was one of the chief engineers on this tunnel project. She, herself, was a graduate civil engineer.

Monk and the lawyer immediately had deep respect for Chick Lancaster. She was apparently a very capable young woman.

Through the night, a booming voice crashed out and reached them. Chick asked, "What in the world is that?"

"That's Renny," said Monk.

"Renny!"

Ham explained that Renny, the engineer in Doc's

crowd, was making a speech to the tunnel men. He was trying to keep them on the job. He was explaining that he was an old friend of Hardrock Hennesey's, and that he believed the little mucker still alive. He would do all he could to solve the mystery that had killed a tunnel worker and a farmer who was well known to everyone at the shaft.

The big workers were listening quietly, convinced that here was a giant of a fellow who got results.

Suddenly the girl gripped Monk's arm.

"Look!" she cried.

Monk and Ham stared. They followed the girl's pointing finger. All they saw was the platform built at the opening to the deep shaft going below ground.

"Look at what?" Monk queried.

"Hardrock. He just went below in the bucket!"

The "bucket," the girl explained, was like a giant pail that could accommodate about eight workmen. It was lowered down the fifteen-hundred-foot shaft at the end of a steel cable.

As Chick explained, "In a few days, they'll have the regular elevator car installed. But, at first, we always use one of these until the shaft walls are lined with cement and rails for an elevator cage."

Monk stared over the railing into the black pit. Far, far down he saw a vague light glowing, one of the few electric bulbs strung up and down the seemingly endless shaft leading into the earth.

"Whew!" he murmured.

"There's nothing to it," the girl explained. "I'll go with you."

That made Monk feel sort of sheepish. He grinned.

"I'll go for you," he said. "Soon as that blasted bucket returns."

They waited. Something seemed to be wrong, for the bucket did not return. A workman, seeing the girl, came running over and explained. "Pete—the operator —is over there at the meeting listening to a fellow named Renwick. There's no one to run this equipment."

That did not seem to stop quick-thinking Chick Lancaster. She indicated the building nearby, where the hoisting machinery was located. "I'll run it," she said.

A few moments later the bucket was at ground level again. Monk climbed in, feeling funny as the steel, barrel-shaped thing swayed beneath his feet. Swayed over a hole fifteen hundred feet deep!

Ham, grinning, announced, "I'd better stay with the girl. She might need me."

Monk exclaimed, "Dangit, I'm gonna—"

But at that moment Ham gave the girl a hand signal from where he stood. She threw a lever and the bucket started down.

Monk, with a start, clutched at the sides of the makeshift car. His breath whistled through his teeth as the shaft walls, black and menacing, zoomed past his gaze.

For Chick Lancaster had failed to mention that the bucket traveled at a speed approaching six hundred feet per minute!

Monk never quite remembered climbing out of the bucket at the base of the shaft. This was all a dream; soon the thing would crash and he would be somewhere in China. He was still so dizzy from effects of the hurtling descent that he staggered around in circles.

Massive rock walls swayed before his vision. Stretching out endlessly to right and left, was the eighteen-foot bore that was the greatest water-carrying project ever constructed.

And here at the base of the shaft, the tunnel proper widened in a mammoth chamber where machinery could be moved and rock that was brought out of the tunnel, unloaded.

It was just as the hairy chemist was regaining his equilibrium that he saw the walking mummy.

He gulped, stared.

"I'm in hell, sure!" Monk gasped.

The man looked like something ageless. He was so thin that it seemed he surely must break in two as his spindle legs moved. A tunnel overhead light revealed his cracked, brown face, that was like withered parchment.

Monk frowned. He had come down here seeking Hardrock Hennesey. He had also expected to find a few muckers or miners down here in the tunnel. But apparently all were above at the meeting led by Renny.

But this fellow, this mummified apparition—

The figure said in a strange voice, "Come! Follow me!"

Monk gave a start, for that voice was like something from the dead.

But he followed.

That was his mistake.

Four individuals moved out from concealment against the rock walls. They piled on hairy Monk. The mummified man disappeared.

Monk swung into action, his powerful fists slamming at ducking heads. Gone was his amazement. These four big men with the ugly faces were something real. They were something you could fight, and so the chemist went to work on them joyously.

Heads snapped on assorted necks. There were grunts of pain. Cries like: "Ouch! Call for help!"

Monk was just getting unlimbered when the four took out in a furious race through the half-dark tunnel. Monk, disgusted, followed.

His short, bowed legs were not quite fast enough to keep up with the escaping four. But he managed to keep them in sight. From his pocket the chemist removed one of the spring-generated flashlights that all the aids of Doc Savage carried.

He switched on the light and could see the running men plainly. And then, abruptly, he couldn't. They had dived into a slight hollow that was a part of the tunnel rock wall.

Monk barged in after them.

And his head slammed against granite and he went down in a heap. Stars exploded. His skull felt like it was split wide open.

Dazedly, Monk felt of the walls. There was nothing except rough rock. No opening. No hide-out. Nothing.

Monk perceived this in the racing seconds before unconsciousness overtook him. The slam of his head against solid rock had been too much for even his tough skull. He sat down and went temporarily to sleep.

But something peculiar, a certain warmness, woke him up. He was wet with perspiration and his lungs felt as though they had inhaled burning, scorching hot air.

He swayed to his feet, gasping. He recalled that as he had chased the four through the tunnel, he had passed a bucket of water placed there for workmen, or perhaps overlooked by a water boy.

He staggered through the oppressive heat, located the bucket, bent down to pick it up—then stared.

The water bucket was empty, whereas a few moments before it had been practically full.

Monk started to mutter, "Golly-wockus! Maybe I'm seein' things! Maybe that bucket didn't stop . . . an' I'm dead!"

He couldn't figure it out.

But what he *could* understand was the thing he saw when his gaze went beyond the water bucket and along the shadowy tunnel. He saw the stuff that trailed slowly toward him like seeking tentacles of doom.

Fog!

Grayish, sort of transparent stuff that spread quickly and silently.

Monk gulped. He recalled Hardrock Hennesey's excited words to Renny over the phone. Fog that burned. Fog that made mummies of men! Hardrock had screamed something about it just after he'd mentioned the package addressed to Doc Savage!

Monk, held petrified for a moment, stared at the opaque, misty stuff. Then he started backing up slowly. A thought hit him even as he did so. If he backed up like this, how would he ever get *out* of the tunnel?

While he was worrying about this, the masked

figure came plunging out of the misty substance and raced toward Monk. He was a man giant in stature; the fact became obvious as he approached. And the mask over his face was some sort of breathing apparatus.

From behind it, a compelling, deep-timbered voice ordered, "Put on this mask. Hurry!"

It was the unusual voice of Doc Savage!

Chapter V

MESSAGE FROM CHICK

Somehow, Monk got into the protective head helmet that was shoved into his hands.

Then Doc Savage was urging him toward the shaft, the single outlet from the tunnel. From behind the mask, he ordered, "We have about one minute to escape with our lives."

Monk started running. But he was still groggy from the crack on his head. He thought he was making good time, but apparently Doc Savage saw need for greater haste. He scooped powerful Monk up in his arms and ran with him. Ran through the hazy gray stuff that seared the hands, that felt like a puff of breath from a dragon's lungs.

Doc Savage carried heavily-built Monk as though he might have been a child. Standing alone, Monk looked like a pretty powerful fellow. But compared to Doc Savage, he now seemed almost puny in stature.

For the bronze man was a physical giant. Veins in his bronze-hued hands stood out like taut cords. The muscles in his neck showed a remarkable strength found in few men. Though his face was shielded by the breathing mask, a glass front showed the unusual bronze features. Doc's hair was of the same color, only somewhat darker.

He ran as easily and as swiftly as though he might have been carrying a rag doll.

They reached the wider opening at the base of the shaft. Doc set Monk down, whipped off his mask.

He said briefly, "That stuff is spreading. Climb into that thing."

Doc had indicated the huge bucket which was used to carry workmen up and down the fifteen-hundred-foot shaftway. Monk tumbled into the thing, pulling off the protective mask, at the same time bubbling over with questions.

"Doc!" he piped in his squeaky voice. "How in blazes did you know I was down here? How did you *get* here?"

"No time for questions," Doc Savage said swiftly. He was in the elevator device beside hairy Monk. He reached out a bronze hand and pulled on a cable that was a signal to those aboveground.

They waited. But nothing happened.

And out of the tunnel behind them something opaque and hazy floated. It appeared like a giant spider's web creeping.

Doc indicated the masks. Monk yanked his back on. From behind his own, Doc Savage said, "The girl —the one named Chick Lancaster—is operating the elevator machinery. She was to wait for the signal."

Monk shuddered, watching the gray stuff that was swiftly floating toward them. Already his hands were seared from passing through just a part of the stuff. He could imagine what would happen if they were completely enveloped by it!

"I hate to admit it," he blurted from behind the mask, "but maybe that girl is crooked!"

Doc said nothing.

And then, without warning, the bucket started upward suddenly. It swiftly hit maximum speed. It almost took the hairy chemist's breath away.

He looked at Doc Savage. But the bronze man was standing as though he might be merely riding in a building elevator to the second floor. His features were calm.

The dizzy flight upward took two and a half

minutes. Monk's eardrums cracked at the changes in pressure. His head whirled.

And then they were climbing out of the thing. It had come to an automatic stop as a "trip" shut off current at the surface landing.

There was no one around. Doc hurriedly led the way to the building that contained the machinery which operated the bucket lift. It, too, was deserted.

Chick Lancaster, the girl, was missing.

It was Doc who found the note that the girl had left for them. It was tucked beside the switchbox located on the wall, and it read:

> We think we have located Hardrock Hennesey. If you find this message, follow to the Yellow River Dam, two miles north of here. We'll be at the superintendent's home there. Ham is accompanying me.

The hastily written note was signed "Chick Lancaster."

Monk looked upset.

"That shyster Ham sure works fast!" he blurted. "No tellin' what he'll tell her about me."

Doc Savage did not comment. His metallic features were expressionless.

Monk suddenly remembered something else. "Where's Renny?" he asked. "He was talkin' to some of the tunnel workers just before I went down in that blasted elevator thing—"

"Renny is still with them," Doc advised. "They have gone to the home of the girl's brother, one of the engineers on this project. It is important to keep the men on the job—regardless of whatever mystery has happened here tonight."

Monk described the mummylike old man he had seen down in the tunnel. He told about the dead man back in the gas station, and of what had been reported before their arrival by Hardrock Hennesey. Something about a farmer who had become a mummified corpse.

The hairy chemist's eyes were wide. "Doc! What the blazes has all that got to do with this tunnel job? Certainly there's no connection!"

The bronze giant was leading the way toward a big limousine parked near the shaft buildings. It was Doc's specially equipped car, a machine that contained bulletproof armor and various scientific devices of the bronze man's own invention. For a moment after Monk spoke, Doc said nothing.

Then he said quietly, "There might be more connection than you think."

Monk puzzled over that for a while. They were in the car now, and Doc took the only road that led north. They passed a road sign that indicated they were on the route to Yellow River Dam.

Monk had imagination. He suddenly blurted, "Doc, you think maybe this tunnel work, this business of boring down there into the earth, might have unearthed some ghosts?"

The bronze man's gaze remained on the road ahead.

"Ghosts?" he prodded.

"Yeah. You take them guys that dig up old tombs and pyramids . . . something always happens to them. They die . . . or get some danged funny disease that nobody can cure. Maybe this is something like that! Goshamighty, there's sure *some* kind of mystery here at this—"

"The mystery at present," Doc put in, "is what was in the package addressed to us. The package Hardrock Hennesey saw in the farmer's car."

"The girl told you when you arrived here?"

Doc nodded.

"Then," Monk said confidently, "as soon as we find Hardrock now, at the dam, we'll know all about it."

"I wonder if Hardrock is the one we'll find," finished Doc, and he lapsed into silence as he drove through the warm night.

The chemist looked at the bronze man swiftly. Doc's comment puzzled him. He could not see where they were going to have any trouble meeting up with

Hardrock Hennesey. The girl's note had said she knew where he now was. It was all very simple.

But there was nothing simple about the carefully arranged trap awaiting Monk and Doc Savage at Yellow River Dam.

The gigantic unit in the water tunnel system sprawled like a black, bottomless crater in the night. For two miles, the dam spread up and down the mountain valley in which it had been built. A great wall had been completed at the lower end of the dam. Across this was a roadway for automobiles; the road was already in use, though the dam itself was not quite completed.

It was beyond this roadway, atop a hill overlooking the dark, gloomy void of concrete and steel framework, that the superintendent's house stood. It was the house that had been mentioned in Chick Lancaster's note. Lights burned on the first floor behind drawn shades.

Inside, in the basement of the house, a group of individuals who appeared like anything but tunnel workers were holding a consultation.

One man consulted his watch. He said, "Doc Savage and that funny-looking guy left the shaft five minutes ago. They're due here any minute."

The speaker had a hawklike face and nervous hands. He looked toward a big man who seemed to be in charge of the group. Other eyes followed his own.

"Everything's set?" the big man asked.

There were affirmative nods.

"Then this'll take care of that Savage guy," said the leader. He grinned.

The leader had a blocky face, big hands and black, piercing eyes. The thing that made him appear twice as big was the long, bulky raincoat which he wore. There seemed to be no logical reason for the raincoat, except that it was black, and perhaps offered a good means of concealment outside in the dark.

The fellow also seemed to be troubled with indigestion.

He was frequently addressed by the others as Pinky. He was about six foot two.

A man suddenly appeared at the top of a flight of stairs that led down into the basement.

"They're here!" he announced in a hushed voice.

The announcement seemed to be a signal for everyone to move toward the stairs. But instead of going up to the first floor, all gathered in a tight knot just below the door leading to the rooms above.

Pinky said, "You've got the super and Hardrock Hennesey all fixed?"

"And how!" replied the one who had joined them. "Both on the living-room floor. Both out cold. Doc and that assistant of his will think they had a fight, and when they go to help them—"

"All right," Pinky rapped. "Quiet!"

Two moments later, a doorbell rang somewhere in the house. It was repeated a moment later.

Then, shortly, there was the sound of footsteps as two men entered the front hallway above. The door behind which the waiting group crouched was right at the end of the hallway, a dozen feet or so from the entrance to the living room.

The footsteps paused in the hallway. Then there came the sound of an exclamation. Monk's words.

"Doc! Lookit! Two guys out cold on the parlor floor!"

After that the waiting group heard footsteps moving into the living room. There followed a sharp crackling sound. A moment later, heavy bodies struck the living-room rug, threshed around a moment. Then —silence.

Pinky grinned. "That's what I call neat," he said. "Taking that bronze guy with his own tricks. We planted them little glass vials in the rug. We'll wait two minutes for the knockout gas to evaporate, then we'll go up."

They waited, each man with a gun in his fist. Though apparently there was going to be no trouble from above, none took chances. As one man said:

"You never can tell about that Doc Savage guy. Wish I had a tommy gun instead of this gat!"

Pinky laughed softly. He belched. "Them two birds will be out cold for an hour," he said.

A moment later, at his signal, all proceeded to the upper hallway. They flung into the living room.

It was deserted.

One of the gunmen started to exclaim, "Say! What the hell happened—"

And then the sharp sputtering sounds came from beneath his feet, from beneath the shoes of his companions. They were firecracker noises followed by puffs of yellow, bilious-looking gassy stuff.

Big Pinky and the others started choking. A couple of the gunmen fell down.

Another happened to stare toward a far corner of the large room. His eyes goggled. He let out a cry of terror.

It was the first time the fellow had ever seen Doc Savage. He was never going to forget it in all his shady life.

At first, the bronze man did not seem unusually large. It was only when he moved toward the confused, staggering mob of gunmen that he seemed to grow in stature. This was made more noticeable when the apelike fellow appeared beside the bronze man.

Compared to Monk, Doc suddenly became a giant. A giant who was perfectly proportioned. The protective head mask that Doc Savage was wearing made him the more startling.

The helmet contained a glass front, and behind this the unusual eyes of Doc Savage seemed to have a compelling, hypnotic effect. Even as the staring gunman swayed before falling, as a result of breathing the anaesthetic gas, he was to long remember those hypnotic eyes. Of a strange flake-gold quality, they seemed to move restlessly, as though continually stirred by tiny winds.

Others saw Doc and the hairy fellow who was beside him. They tried to get up their guns, to fire at the two. But their arms were suddenly sluggish with leaden weight, and the guns sagged and they all started falling down.

Only Pinky, the big leader in the long raincoat, had had presence of mind enough to leap backward when the gas pellets started exploding beneath his feet.

He streaked through the front hallway, reached the outer door and slammed out into the night.

Monk followed, looking like some sort of apish monster in his face mask.

But by the time Monk reached the front porch, the big man had faded into the gloom somewhere along the walls of the mammoth dam. The purpose of his long, dark raincoat was obvious. It blended perfectly with the night.

Monk yanked from beneath his coat a peculiar-looking automatic pistol with a drumlike magazine. It was one of the mercy pistols that all Doc Savage aids carried. The weapon made bull-fiddle roars in the quiet night as Monk pressed the trigger.

He aimed the gun in the general direction that the escaping man had taken.

Beside him, his mask now off, Doc Savage said quietly, "He's probably escaped. We'd better take care of these others."

But the assorted thugs lying on the living-room floor seemed to be well taken care of. All but one were asleep. The man who wasn't was out in the hallway staggering around. He stared out of bleared eyes as Doc and Monk came back into the house.

He tried to blurt, "What . . . how—"

Doc said, "You fellows should have checked more carefully on the girl's handwriting before leaving that note."

Monk indicated a room across the hallway. The door to the room was closed.

"We'd better see if Hardrock Hennesey is all right," the chemist suggested.

He and the bronze man had not put on their gas masks again, for the yellowish substance had now disappeared. Its effectiveness only lasted a moment or so.

Doc nodded, glancing at the fellow who was still swaying on his feet before them.

Monk grinned. He said to the man, "Planting

them danged gas pellets was a bright idea, fella. Only we just changed them around a little bit so *you'd* get them instead of us!"

Then he let go with a fist that put the man asleep temporarily. Monk carried the man into the living room and dumped him beside his pals.

From the doorway of the room that had been closed across the hall, a thin, leathery-faced man with intense gray eyes appeared. His jaw stuck out like a block of cement and he looked like a taut length of tough piano wire.

Hardrock Hennesey!

Hardrock Hennesey growled, "Where's the damned cuss who slugged me?"

Chapter VI

"J. L."

Hardrock Hennesey was the sort of individual who had knocked around the universe long enough to become accustomed to surprises.

And so he looked Monk over briefly. He made no comments about the chemist's homely features. Hardrock, himself, would have taken no beauty prizes.

He did, however, stare at Doc Savage for a moment. The bronze man's remarkable physique caused Hardrock Hennesey's intense gray eyes to widen imperceptibly. But all he said was:

"Thanks for the help, Doc Savage. How the hell did you guys work it?" He waved a hand toward the living room. "Those birds had a nice trap all set for you."

"That," the bronze man explained, "was quite evident from the forged handwriting in Chick Lancaster's note. So we merely rearranged the gas pellets that had been planted in the rug. We put you and the other man in a safe spot, and then waited for results after pretending we had fallen down and been knocked out."

Hardrock shook his head. "Not bad, not bad," he commented.

He led the way back into the room from which he'd appeared. It was a dining room in which Doc and Monk had placed Hardrock and the dam superintendent upon finding them unconscious in the living room.

The superintendent was a tall, wiry man with sun-burned features. He was just struggling to his feet when they came into the room.

Hardrock explained that the two persons with him were Doc Savage and a fellow named Monk. It appeared the super's name was Flynn, and he was still mystified as to why he and Hardrock Hennesey had been seized by the gunmen.

Doc directed the tying up of the unconscious men while he made a brief explanation.

"It is obvious," he said, "that someone has an idea that Hardrock Hennesey, here, knows something about a mystery which seems to be centered with this tunnel project."

The hard-boiled little tunnel worker straightened up from where he was tying up a man.

"The hell you say!" he blurted. His eyes were puzzled. "Sure, some damn funny things happened to-night, but that doesn't say they have anything to do with this tunnel job. If they do, I don't know what it's all about."

"The package might explain a whole lot of things," said Doc.

"Package?"

"The package you found in the farmer's car, addressed to me."

Hardrock jumped. "That's right. Almost forgot about it. But it was gone when I came back!"

"Any idea where it might be?"

The mucker's ageless, leathery face was thoughtful.

"Hell, no!"

Flynn, the superintendent, also had a question.

"How," he wanted to know, "do you happen to be involved in this thing, Doc Savage?"

Monk, too, had a question. His small, bright eyes swung on the bronze man.

"Blazes, Doc!" he piped shrilly. "That's something I was gonna ask you, too? How did you know what was going on up at this blasted place?"

For a brief instant, the bronze man's flake-gold eyes met Monk's. The others missed the glance. But the chemist suddenly understood that there would be an explanation later, when they were alone.

Doc said, "The first thing to do is lock these captives up. We will question them later."

Tall, bony Flynn stepped to a phone, put through a call to the special police. It was this division of the police that did patrol duty on the various shafts in the great tunnel project.

Leaving Flynn to take charge of the trussed-up captives, Doc led the way back to where he had parked his car. He and Monk were accompanied by tough little Hardrock Hennesey.

Hardrock rapped, "By damn, I'm mad!" He massaged a bruise that was on the side of his protruding jaw. "Wait'll I get hold of the geezer that conked me!"

Monk had opened the car door. He turned.

"While you're waiting," he remarked, "maybe you can tell us some more about what happened?"

Hardrock Hennesey had suddenly stiffened. "Say!" he exploded.

"Well?" Monk prodded, watching the tunnel man.

Hardrock was tugging at something in his pocket. "Here's something I *did* find." His gaze swung to the bronze man. "Maybe you'll be interested in it, Doc Savage."

Monk had opened the rear door of Doc's sedan, and the man squatted on the floor there raised up and shoved the gun muzzle in the hairy chemist's face.

"Let's get interested in *this!*" he snarled.

In the moment that the shadowy figure spoke, Doc Savage whirled into blinding motion. His swinging arm knocked Monk to one side. His left hand caught Hardrock Hennesey in the same instant and pushed him into a tumbling heap down beside the car.

The gun blasted almost in the bronze giant's face.

But in reality, the shot was lower than that, and the slug hit the bulletproof garment that Doc Savage was wearing beneath his clothing. It merely staggered Doc Savage a little.

Astounded, the gunman within the car had been disconcerted for a moment. In that second Doc Savage slapped the gun from the man's fist, seized him by the neck, dragged him out onto the ground.

Monk, howling with rage, took over.

Though the captive was well over six feet, solid and as strong as a bull, hairy Monk slapped the man around until he was weaving on his feet.

The fellow fell down. Monk picked him up, hit him again, held him from falling and snorted, "Brother, now you're gonna answer a few questions!"

The car headlamps were turned on and the captive dragged around in front of the machine.

Monk swore. "You!" he piped.

It was Pinky, the big fellow in the long raincoat. He glared at the chemist, then belched.

Hardrock Hennesey let out a yell and leaped for Pinky.

"*That's* the punk who slugged me!" Hardrock said. "Let me—"

Doc Savage warned, "Wait! Perhaps this fellow can answer some of our questions."

The bronze man's unusual eyes were trained on the captive, who stood a little apart from them, distinctively revealed by the headlamp glare.

His lips curled. "Nuts!" he said.

Monk grinned.

"Wait a minute, Doc," he started to say. "I'm just gonna—"

The shot from up the hillside beside them was a flat, menacing sound in the hot night. Everyone whirled, but above them there was only the uncertain gloom of the embankment that rose for perhaps a hundred feet above the newly constructed dam.

It sounded like the crack of a rifle, and it was not repeated. But all knew that anyone could have hidden up there at the top of the embankment, fired the shot, then slid off into the night.

Each had jumped clear of the headlights' revealing glow. Monk and Hardrock Hennesey had started to dive toward the hillside. Then they drew up short at the sound that suddenly floated in the night air.

It was a trilling—soft, almost musical; it was difficult to locate the source of the unusual tone.

But Monk recognized it. It was an unconscious thing the bronze man did in moments of mental stress —or perhaps surprise.

Monk whirled toward Doc—and stared.

Their captive, the big, sneering fellow known as Pinky, was swaying back and forth like a man dizzy with the heat. Even as Monk watched, Pinky's legs seemed to give out beneath him and he collapsed to his knees. He was clutching his stomach. From his knees he lurched forward onto his face, groaned once, then lay still.

Doc Savage bent forward. Light revealed the red liquid on the fallen man's back. The rifle slug had entered there, gone clean through the big man's body. He was dead.

Doc Savage straightened, ordered, "Monk, carry him back to the house. Tell Flynn what happened. Then hurry back here."

A quick search of the dead man's pockets revealed that he carried nothing that would identify him—or show for whom he was working.

While Monk was gone, Doc Savage and Hardrock Hennesey climbed the hillside, searched for any clue to Pinky's slayer. Fifty feet back from the top of the embankment, they found where a car had been parked. The tire marks of the machine showed that the rubber was too well worn to leave any kind of identifying tracks. There was no trace of the car or the one who had driven it.

Five minutes later, when Monk had returned, they were driving back toward Shaft 9.

Doc, at the wheel of the car, turned to Hardrock Hennesey. "You said there was something you had found," he prodded. "What?"

Hardrock nodded, reached into his pocket. What he brought out was something embedded in a piece of rocklike substance. It was quite hideous.

It was the shape of a hand, and it had claws.

Doc had stopped the car momentarily. He was examining the object as Hardrock explained.

"Found that down in Shaft 9," Hardrock said. "It's a claw that can be used to slip over the hand. Like brass knuckles, in a way, but damned if I ever seen anything quite like that."

It was Doc who said, "A form of fighting weapon used hundreds of years ago." He looked briefly at Hardrock. "You say you found it down in the tunnel?"

The tough little mucker jerked his head.

"Damned right I did. An' something else."

"What?" Monk demanded.

"Evidence that the new tunnel has passed through something damned peculiar down there!" Hardrock offered. "Something that looks like an old ocean floor. People must have lived down there thousands of years ago."

Monk scratched his head. "You been drinking?" he prodded.

Hardrock snorted.

"Wish I had!" the mucker exclaimed. "Wait'll I show you some other stuff I found."

They proceeded to Shaft 9. They located Renny, and the giant-sized engineer reported, "I think I've got the workmen talked into returning to their jobs. But not until morning. They're all upset by what's happened tonight."

Monk stared around. "But where are they now?"

Renny looked worried.

"Searching for the girl," he announced in his booming voice. "She's missing."

Hardrock Hennesey stuck out his jaw. "If anything happens to Chick, I'll cut the throat of the guy—"

Monk's eyes had narrowed. "Hey!" he exclaimed. "Is Ham still with her?"

"He was," Renny replied.

Hardrock frowned. "Who's this guy Ham?" he demanded.

"A shyster!" hairy Monk announced. "Betcha he's already got that girl Chick convinced—"

Doc Savage interrupted with, "Renny can stay up here and operate the lift machinery. Also, he can watch for the girl or Ham. We'd better get started."

Just as they reached the huge bucket that would lower them swiftly below ground, Monk remembered the mysterious gray stuff that was like fog, the thing they had encountered down in the tunnel.

He mentioned it to Doc.

But Doc Savage indicated the masks he had brought along from his car. "We'll have to take that chance," he said.

Hardrock was already in the bucket with Doc Savage. Monk followed, looking somewhat worried.

He said, "Doc, I think we're taking an awful—"

The bronze man had just straightened up from picking up something off the floor of the shaft lift. What he held was a girl's small handkerchief. In one corner were the two initials, "J. L."

"Jane!" Hardrock Hennesey cried.

"Jane who?" Monk asked.

"Lancaster. That's Chick's handkerchief. Her correct name is Jane!"

Monk grinned. He no longer appeared worried about going below.

"Come on," he piped, "I just want to see that blasted shyster Ham!"

But what they were to find was something else again.

Chapter VII

STRANGE WORLD

At the base of the great shaft, they stood listening a few moments. They had seen no trace of the peculiar grayish fog upon stepping from the steel bucket.

There was something awesome, something tremendous, about being down here fifteen hundred feet beneath the earth surface. Curved walls hemmed them in. The tunnel stretched right and left like the yawning, dark mouth of a Gargantuan serpent.

Except for the distant whisper of air being pumped down through the ventilating system, there was an abysmal silence, profound, sort of chilling.

Monk shrugged off the creepy feeling, grinned and said, "Well, Hardrock, where do we start looking for the rest of this antique claw of yours?"

Hardrock Hennesey had been listening intently. He moved to the tunnel wall, pressed his ear flat against the surface for a moment. His leathery face screwed up and he appeared thoughtful.

"Funny!" he commented.

Monk watched him. "What's funny?"

"I don't think there's anybody down here," Hardrock said. He looked at Doc Savage. "And yet there was Chick's handkerchief!"

Monk muttered, "Wait'll I get that guy Ham!"

Doc said nothing for a moment. Then, quietly, "Why would the girl come down here?"

Hardrock Hennesey shrugged. "She has the run of this place. Maybe she and that Ham discovered something. Or"—Hardrock's intense gray eyes looked worried—"maybe they've been tricked!"

"That occurred to me," was Doc's significant remark.

It was a toss-up as to which way they should go. As Hardrock explained, "I was talking to one of the miners earlier. The south bore from here extends three miles; the north bore almost four. If they *are* down here, they might have gone either way."

Doc nodded. "Which way to the place where you found this?"

The bronze man indicated the hand with the claw, which the little tunnel worker had turned over to him.

"Back here," Hardrock said, indicating the north extension of the tunnel behind them.

Doc suggested that they might as well proceed that way first. At least, they would investigate the thing Hardrock Hennesey had located.

The bronze man was using one of his flashlights, though the tunnel itself was dimly lighted by the electric bulbs. Doc's eyes explored the floor of the big tunnel as they walked along.

Behind them and before them, their footsteps made weird sounds as they echoed and reverberated through the tunnel. When anyone spoke, the words went trailing away into the distance, echoing like strange voices from a nether world.

Each man carried a gas mask, held ready in case the uncanny-looking fog should be seen again. But they saw no trace of it.

As Hardrock explained, "Dammit, I've been working in tunnels for thirty years. Never saw anything quite like it either above or belowground. You could see through it, and yet you couldn't. You just imagined you could!"

Doc Savage said nothing. His alert eyes were constantly probing ahead. His ears were sharp for the slightest foreign sound.

Once Monk exclaimed, "Blazes! This looks about where I slammed my head into that blasted wall. Wait a minute!"

The chemist moved to the side of the tunnel,

started a search. He remembered where he had seen the running thugs. He looked around for several moments as Doc and Hardrock Hennesey waited.

Scratching his head, he joined them again. "Maybe I was having hallucinations!" Monk remarked.

They continued. They covered perhaps a mile of underground passageway. They saw nothing, heard no one moving ahead.

It was just about this point that Doc Savage picked up the object off the tunnel floor.

Monk stared. "Gollywockus!" he piped.

Hardrock Hennesey squinted and couldn't believe his eyes.

What Doc Savage held was a spearlike weapon that was like nothing Monk had ever seen. It was made of stone that was harder than flint. It was crude. It looked like a weapon that might have been used in the era of cliff dwellers.

Doc held the spear up before the flashlight glare, and all saw what he indicated.

There was blood on the head of the spear, and it was still moist.

Doc Savage stood looking at the strange weapon, his eyebrows slightly knitted together. It was Hardrock who said:

"Somebody's been struck—and with *that!*" His eyes were wide. "But who—what *kind* of person would use an implement like that?"

Monk blurted, "Maybe a cave dweller!"

"Don't be crazy!" Hardrock started to say. And them he stared, his eyes getting wider. "Say! Do you really think—"

Doc interrupted them.

"Perhaps we should look farther into the tunnel," he suggested.

Monk was first to lead the way. His homely features were worried-looking. He piped shrilly, "Blast it! Maybe Ham and the girl are hurt!"

That appeared to be the thought of all as they quickened their pace and hurried through the seemingly endless eighteen-foot bore that passed through the earth. A muck-car track stretched through the entire length.

Even at the fast pace they were traveling, it was some time before they reached the northern end of the bore. Then they came upon the mucking machines and equipment near the tunnel head. There was evidence that the miners and muckers who had worked here had walked off the job in a hurry. A "powder monkey" had left a case of dynamite lying dangerously in the open, near the tracks where the muck cars passed. Drills and jackhammers had been dropped and lay carelessly about.

In the tunnel head itself, work had been hastily stopped, and the huge platform where the drillers had been working was strewn with tools.

Strangely, they had passed no one, seen no moving thing.

Monk stared at Doc Savage. He exclaimed, "Goshamighty, *somebody* musta got hurt with that spear. But where is he? An' who *did* it?"

Apparently there was no answer for that.

Doc Savage moved among the machinery and equipment located here at the tunnel head. His eyes flashed over things briefly. He obviously found nothing that startled him.

Doc's eyes were thoughtful, though, when he came back to Hardrock and Monk. He looked at the little tunnel worker.

"You were going to show us where you found that hand with the claw," Doc reminded.

Hardrock gave a slight start. "That's right!" he exclaimed. "Forgot all about it when we found that spear. Come on."

He led the way back through the tunnel bore. Following him, Monk gave the bronze man a questioning glance. The glance said that perhaps this Hardrock Hennesey was not a person to be trusted.

But the expression in the bronze giant's eyes told Monk nothing.

A quarter of a mile back through the tunnel,

Hardrock paused, studying the rock walls. This was a section that had not yet been cemented over, as the entire tunnel would be before completion.

"Let's have that light," Hardrock asked, indicating Doc's flashlight.

Taking it, he sprayed the powerful light ray up along the curved wall. About on a level with his head, he held the light beam steady for a moment on the wall surface. Then he moved it back and forth slowly in a horizontal plane.

"Do you see that?" he prodded.

Doc Savage had stepped closer. He was examining the vein of earth revealed by the moving light. Then he was digging into the rock substance with his powerful fingers.

A piece of stuff that looked like sand turned to rock came loose. The bronze man studied it intently. A bit of substance crumbled beneath the great strength of his crushing fingers. Something like a small, petrified shell dropped into the bronze giant's palm.

Doc said thoughtfully, "It appears that, hundreds of years ago, this level down here was originally the earth's surface. This was the original sea level."

Hardrock Hennesey jerked his head. "That's what I figured!" he cried. "And this is just about where I found the claw thing."

Monk was a chemist, not an archaeologist. He stared, blurted a question.

"Doc! You mean people used to *live* here in this blasted place?"

"When it was the earth's surface," Doc said. "That was before the Glacial period, before this whole area was changed by some earth movement."

Monk breathed, "Golly!"

Hardrock put in, "They've found such a situation on other water-tunnel jobs. On one leading into New York City, down about a thousand feet they found where elm trees—or trees like them—had once been growing. People must have lived there at one time."

Monk looked at the clawed-hand thing pro-

truding from the bronze man's pocket, and his little
eyes bulged.

"Kind of spooky!" he said.

But not more spine-chilling than the horrible,
weird cry that came from somewhere ahead of them.
Drifting through the miles of underground tunnel, it
gained volume, was magnified into a dreadful scream
of terror.

It was Hardrock Hennesey who said in almost a
whisper, "It ... it sounds like a guy ... *dying!*"

They ran for ten minutes toward the source of
the cry. The sound came once again, closer this time.
There seemed to be more of a dreadful wail to the
sound.

Monk was sweat-soaked. He wiped at his brow
as he ran. "Whew!" he complained. "Thought it was
cool down here a little while ago. But I'm dang-blasted
hot now!"

Even the bronze man's metallic features were
beaded with moisture, though Doc showed no other
effect of the race through the tunnel. He was well
ahead of the others. And thus it was that he was
first to draw up short and call out a warning.

"Watch out!" Doc Savage rapped.

Monk and Hardrock Hennesey shortly flung to a
stop behind him. Both stared ahead.

Monk, puzzled, piped shrilly, "What is it? I don't
see anything."

"Watch!" said Doc.

And then, slowly, the thing became obvious to
the others. Monk squinted, and Hardrock Hennesey
seemed to give a slight shudder.

He cried, "The fog!"

It didn't look like a fog, at first. Drifting slowly,
sort of translucent, the stuff might have been a mirage.
It floated like thin morning mist on a mountain top.

Monk's small eyes were straining. He suddenly
yelled. "Doc! There's somebody *moving* in that stuff!"

But Doc Savage had already seen. He whipped
out an order.

"Hold your gas masks in readiness!"

The bronze man, his own mask in his hand, moved forward with blurred speed.

And as suddenly he stopped, as though he had smashed into a solid wall of rock. He backed up slowly. Ahead of him, the opaque substance slowly became a solid mass of grayness.

Doc motioned Monk and Hardrock Hennesey back. All were aware now of an extreme heat that beat against their faces, that caused their hands to smart. The heat fast grew more intense.

They kept moving backward, staring, and Monk understood why he had been perspiring so a moment earlier. It was *this*—some uncanny thing that was unapproachable.

Hardrock cried, "It . . . it was like that where the farmer died. It's the same thing!"

Doc Savage's eyes were intent. They tried again to locate the object that he had seen moving within the mass. But he could not see beyond the gray pall.

They all heard the scream.

Frantic, utterly terrible, it held them rigid a moment. And then the stuff was pressing closer, driving them still farther backward. They were helpless before its searing heat.

They were helpless to aid whoever was *within* that death fog.

It was Hardrock Hennesey who yelled. "Somebody's dying in there!"

Doc did not answer. He made an attempt to move forward, but was literally hurled back by the fiery heat that lay ahead.

And then, for the first time, Hardrock Hennesey showed fear. He grabbed the bronze man's arm, pointed toward the gray wall that blocked them off.

"Listen!" he screamed. "What'll we do. That's *the only way out of here!*"

Monk rapped, "As if we don't know it!"

It was obvious that they were trapped.

Chapter VIII

ESCAPE

The gray-looking substance continued to spread, and Doc Savage, Monk and Hardrock Hennesey were forced to keep retreating. But after a while the fog stopped moving, remaining motionless in the air. It hung there like smoke trapped in a small pipe.

The bronze man's eyes flickered. "Perhaps now," he said quietly, "we can escape."

Monk gulped. "Escape! How? Not through that stuff!"

Doc directed that the two were to wait for him. They were to remain clear of the death fog. He would return as quickly as possible.

Doc left them, running back toward the northern end of the tunnel.

"What's he going to do?" Hardrock Hennesey asked, worried.

Monk shrugged. "No tellin' what Doc's ever going to do. We'll just have to wait."

They waited in grim silence, their eyes on the motionless gray fog, a hundred feet down the tunnel away from them.

Once Monk remarked, "I'm gonna blast that guy if we ever get outta here!"

"Who?"

"Ham. Betcha he's already got a date with that Chick Lancaster!"

Hardrock said nothing. He looked at Monk, scowled. They sat there with their chins cupped in their hands and thought about dying. Neither could see how they could possibly escape from here.

Doc Savage's return gave them both somewhat of a start.

It did not seem possible that the bronze man could have run to the tunnel head and back so swiftly. Doc was not even breathing hard.

But a rigid, two-hour daily set of scientific exercises kept the bronze giant in perfect condition at all times. The exercises had been followed since childhood. In fact, the bronze man's entire life was the result of scientific training.

Hardrock Hennesey jumped up and stared at the object the bronze man was carrying. "What're you going to do with that?" he prodded.

For answer, Doc passed a length of wire to the hard-boiled little tunnel man. "Get this ready," he directed swiftly.

What Doc held was a stick of dynamite. Hardrock was preparing the fuse and wire that would be strung to that single piece of dynamite.

Monk looked worried.

"Blazes!" he piped. "You'll blow us to hell and gone, Doc!"

"There's hardly enough here for that," explained Doc.

Ordering them to stand back, and putting on his mask, Doc ran forward toward the fog screen that blocked them in the tunnel. He approached as close as possible to the stuff, set the dynamite stick, played out the wire as he returned.

Then he ordered, "You'd better lie down."

In the next moment, Doc set off the blast.

For seconds afterward, Monk was certain that the tunnel walls were smashing down all around them. But then he discovered it was only the terrific racket shattering against his eardrums. The detonation went rolling back and forth through the bore. Dust blinded their eyes. And then, finally, there was silence.

They stared toward the fog stuff.

It was gone. The tunnel was clear.

Doc Savage led the way. They passed what had once been the body of a man. Doc Savage motioned them on, as he paused momentarily to examine the victim.

There was not the slightest chance of recognition.

The man's head, legs and arms were missing as a result of the explosion. But there was enough of his clothing left to reveal that he must have been a tunnel worker, probably sent down here to look for them, but who had been caught in the death mist.

Ten minutes later they were aboveground.

And there, with giant Renny, they found Chick Lancaster and well-dressed Ham.

Monk howled with rage.

"You blasted shyster! What's the idea of walking out on me?"

Ham smiled coolly. With him were the two pets, Habeas and Chemistry.

"Who ran out on *who?*" Ham demanded. He smiled fondly at the girl. "I've been helping Chick, here, search for Hardrock."

The girl's pretty blue-green eyes, seeing Monk's frown, looked worried. She touched Ham's arm.

"Careful," she cautioned. "He has a mean look on his face!"

The lawyer grimaced. "That's no mean look," he said, "that's his face!"

Doc Savage had been talking to Renny and Hardrock Hennesey. He left them to come over to the girl.

Chick Lancaster's pretty face was suddenly flushed, and she was looking at the giant bronze man out of admiring eyes. All women fell hard the first time they ever met Doc Savage. All learned, later, that Doc avoided falling in love with a girl.

It wasn't because he wasn't human, or because he didn't have a heart. For Doc, with all his scientific training, had as much feeling as the next man. But he controlled those emotions. He believed that because of his dangerous career—that of righting wrongs and punishing evildoers—he should never ask a girl to share that existence with him.

And so, now, he merely nodded to lovely Chick Lancaster and said, "We have been trying to find you. There is something which you can explain."

The red-haired girl gave a little sigh. She felt

suddenly somewhat self-conscious standing before this unusual person.

"Explain?" she asked. "Explain what?"

"Why you wrote to the governor of this State?"

Monk and Ham looked quickly at the bronze man. This was the first they had heard about Doc Savage having previous information about Chick Lancaster.

The girl was startled.

"You . . . knew . . . *that?*" she said.

Doc nodded. He turned his steady gaze to Monk. "That's why the phony note from Pinky and his gang did not fool me. It was not in this girl's handwriting."

Monk looked puzzled.

"But how did you get hold of *her* letter, Doc?" he asked.

"From the governor of the State. It was sent to me." Doc looked back at Chick. "You wrote to the governor telling him of trouble that was happening here. You hinted at something mysterious."

Monk got in another question before the girl could reply.

"Doc, you mean the governor *asked* you to investigate?"

Doc nodded again. "The request," he said, "was sent to me several days ago."

It was something that surprised everyone. It convinced them that there was something of utmost importance connected with the mystery. But what, they did not yet know.

Doc was waiting for the girl's answer. She suddenly stared past them all, looked at the man who was approaching. She said:

"Perhaps my brother can explain better than I."

Raymond Lancaster was a man about forty, with flame-red hair and freckles, and eyes that were as sharp as flint steel. For obvious reasons, he was usually called Reds. He was one of the leading engineers on this new water-tunnel job.

Reds Lancaster had already met big Renny, who literally towered above the man's small, wiry figure. Lancaster was introduced to the others, informed of

Doc Savage's request. He suggested that all adjourn to one of the nearby buildings.

A few moments later, he was explaining:

"Trouble started as soon as we began work on the dam."

"What dam?" Monk put in. He was holding Habeas in one arm, scratching the pig's ear with his hand.

"Yellow River Dam. There were accidents. More than the usual amount." Reds Lancaster, as he talked, played with some sort of chain that held an engineering society key. The chain dangled from the pocket of his expensive whipcord breeches. He was dressed in similar fashion to his sister, Chick Lancaster. "But accidents are a thing you can try to prevent. They are something real."

He stopped jiggling the chain, and the key on it hung straight down, motionless. "But this mystery that happened tonight, this other thing . . . well, it's uncanny. How *can* you fight a thing like that?"

Doc asked: "Have you any theories at all?"

The wiry, alert little engineer was thoughtful a moment. Then he jerked his head. "Yes."

"What?"

"I think it is a direct blow at the governor of this State. I think the whole thing has something to do with him. Call it a menace against his career. Someone is trying to ruin him."

Ham, Monk, Hardrock Hennesey and big Renny stared at the redheaded engineer.

Ham said sharply, "That doesn't make sense! What has the appearance of a mysterious fog, the finding of mummified men got to do with the governor?"

"That," said Reds Lancaster quietly, "is what we have to figure out." His eyes looked suddenly tired. "This stuff about mummies and wierd fogs is nonsense. It *has* to be!"

Monk snorted suddenly. "Yeah?" he demanded shrilly. "Well, brother, just wait until *you* get into some of that stuff!"

Someone looked at Hardrock Hennesey. "How about it, Hardrock? You had a narrow escape?"

All had heard by now about the tough little tunnel worker being trapped by the fog at the gas station. Hardrock had not explained how he had escaped death at that time.

He took a hitch at the overalls that were too large for him, said, "Pinky and those mugs of his grabbed me just before I almost burned up from the heat of that stuff. They put my clothes on that dead farmer's body and left him there in my place. They wanted to make it look like it was me."

He indicated the clothes he was wearing. "That's why I'm wearing that dead guy's clothes."

"Why did they want you?" Ham put in.

"Because they thought I had a package that had been addressed to Doc Savage."

Monk frowned. "Didn't *they* have it?"

Hardrock shook his head.

"Hell, no! It's just disappeared, and no one knows where it is."

Everyone had suddenly started talking at once. It was the bronze man's voice that halted them.

"Just a minute," he said quietly.

He looked at Renny. "Monk and Ham will remain with you. Get all workmen back on their jobs first thing this morning. You might call in the mine police to help patrol the tunnels and shafts. Hardrock can help. Perhaps he can learn something."

Doc looked at the engineer, Reds Lancaster. "You'll co-operate?"

"Certainly. We're losing thousands of dollars a day on this job. We've got to find out what's wrong!"

Renny said in his booming voice, "What are you going to do, Doc?"

"It appears," said the bronze man, "that an interview with the governor might be advisable. I should be back here by tomorrow."

Doc explained a few more things he wished his aids to do. He started for the door.

Someone exclaimed, "Where's the girl?"

Chick Lancaster, it turned out, had left. No one knew where she had gone.

Doc Savage went out into the cool, damp air of early morning. Gray sky was showing in the east, beyond the buildings of Shaft 9.

He went back to his big limousine and swung open the door. He had a long drive ahead, and there was need for hurry.

Chick Lancaster, looking bright and excited, sat in the front seat of the bronze man's car.

She said, "I'm going with you. There's something you should know about."

Chapter IX

TRAIL TO TROUBLE

Approximately five miles north of Yellow River Dam, Doc Savage became aware that another car was following him and the girl.

For the past mile they had been winding through the narrow, steep grades that passed over mountainous country which cut off a valley beyond. It was necessary to reach that valley before the main State road would be encountered. Once reached, the main highway should take them to the capitol in two or three hours.

But now, through the trees behind them, Doc caught an occasional glimpse of the trailing car. He picked up speed. The other car did likewise. He slowed down. The trailing car fell back.

Doc looked at Chick Lancaster and said quietly. "We might have a little trouble, unless you can stand a lot of speed."

"Trouble?"

The bronze man nodded to the rear-view mirror. "We are being trailed."

For two long moments, the girl's blue-green eyes watched the mirror. Then she spoke quietly.

"I think you're right."

Threat of danger didn't seem to terrify this girl as it might some women.

"We can get away from them," Doc said confidently, and he opened the car up.

And what Chick Lancaster observed in the next few moments was a demonstration of driving that astounded her. The road wound and reversed and dipped up and down steep grades. Doc drove almost with relaxation, and yet at speeds that were terrific.

Ten minutes later, the girl looked across at him, grinned and commented, "That's that. We've lost them."

They were now climbing an unusually steep grade that swung over the last remaining hillside before the valley beyond.

Doc started to say, "Someone apparently—"

He paused, his gaze flicking to the dashboard of the car. The car was slowing. It sputtered, came to a stop part way up the hill.

Chick Lancaster's eyes were wide. She had followed the bronze man's gaze to the dashboard needle indicator.

"We're out of gas!" she exclaimed.

"It seems," Doc added, "that someone figured it out carefully. They left just enough gas in the tank so that we would get stalled in this hilly country."

Behind them, at the start of the hill, a car motor roared. It was the sedan that had been following them.

Doc, tense, was suddenly giving swift directions to the girl. As he talked, he yanked up door handles that locked the doors from inside. He did this to all but the door beside him.

"You'll remain in the car," Doc said hurriedly. "There is no possible way they can reach you. You'll be safe."

"But—"

"I'll be back."

Doc Savage reached into a compartment that was located in the dash. He removed a package that was about the size of a one-pound box of chocolates. Slipping the package beneath his coat, he stepped out of the car.

For the first time, the red-haired girl looked scared.

"Please!" she exclaimed.

Doc's words were clipped. "Lock the door after me!" he ordered. "You'll not be harmed. *Don't try to leave the car.*"

He slammed the door behind him, heard the door handle lock as the girl pushed it up from inside.

He also heard the slugs that whined close as he disappeared into the surrounding woods.

Heads were protruding from the big sedan. A man was aiming a pistol and firing in the direction the bronze giant had taken.

The driver of the trailing car—a beefy fellow with a heavy, unshaven face—brought the machine to a stop fifty feet beyond the bronze man's car.

He said, "What the hell!"

There were four other men in the machine beside the driver. They looked like the kind of individuals employed in dock strikes.

All were carrying guns, and all raced toward the bronze man's car.

The beefy man laughed harshly. "Some guy, this Doc Savage. He ran off and left the dame!"

He grabbed the car-door handle. Then he stared. The handle would not budge.

He rapped on the window, glaring at the girl seated inside the machine. "Open up!"

For answer, Chick Lancaster coolly thumbed her nose at the big fellow who needed a shave.

With a snort of rage, the big man backed off, raised his gun and fired at the car window. He fired high enough that the shot would go over the girl's head, but at least it would scare her into unlocking the car doors.

Instead, the five thugs themselves got a shock. The tiniest of marks appeared on the window as a result of the slug striking. The glass did not even web.

The big leader tried shooting at another window. He got the same results.

With a curse, he waved a fist at the girl inside the car.

She merely returned his glare.

Suddenly, one of the other men grabbed the burly fellow's arm. "Hey!" he yelled. "Maybe this is a trick. They say that Doc Savage is pretty smart."

That seemed to hold them all rigid. They swung, stared toward the woods where Doc Savage had vanished.

"Spread out!" the leader rapped. "That bronze guy's in there *some* place. Get him!"

With guns held ready, all five men advanced on the woods acrosss the road. Shortly they disappeared beneath the enshrouding foliage.

From behind the protection of the bulletproof car windows, Chick Lancaster watched.

And five minutes later she heard the roar of guns and the yelling and the wild trampling of underbrush. Men came tumbling out onto the road, piled back into the sedan parked behind Doc's car. The burly-looking fellow was last to appear. He leaped behind the wheel of the car, got the motor started, and almost yanked out the clutch as he sent the car racing up the hill.

None of the men seemed any longer interested in Chick Lancaster. The only thing that apparently worried them was to escape with their lives.

A moment later, black, dense smoke billowed out of the woods at the point where the five men had emerged. It was blinding stuff that shut off Chick Lancaster's view of the spot.

As she stared, a figure appeared out of the black cloud.

It was Doc Savage.

The girl opened the car door, exclaimed. "Mercy! What has happened?"

"They thought the smoke things were bombs," Doc said. "We have succeeded in reversing the game of trailing one another."

"Trailing?" The girl's pretty eyes were puzzled. "You mean you are going to trail *them?*"

Doc nodded. He was now busy taking a two-gallon can from the rear section of the limousine. It was a can of gasoline.

Chick Lancaster climbed out and watched Doc Savage as he dumped the gas into the tank.

"But how?" she demanded. "How do you ever expect to trail them? They'll be miles from here by the time we get to the State road and get more gas."

Doc finished dumping in the gas, put the can away, climbed behind the wheel. From beneath the dashboard of the car he swung out what looked like a small aërial direction-finder. He turned a switch, waited a moment, then said, "Listen."

The series of signals came from a small boxlike affair located near the small aërial. As Doc Savage started up the car he explained:

"Those signals are coming from a small shortwave transmitter placed in their car. We should be able to trail them."

Amazement was mirrored in the blue-green depths of the girl's wide eyes.

"But how in the world did you work that?"

"While they were trying to get into this car, the device was planted in their own. In the trunk on the rear."

Chick Lancaster recalled the package Doc had removed before leaving the car.

"The candy box?"

"Yes."

Chick Lancaster sat back on the seat and heard the steady signals coming from the car far ahead and decided that this bronze man was a fellow worth knowing.

Factory whistles were blowing for the noon lunch hour when Doc Savage passed through the outskirts of the State capital. The steady stream of signals were still coming from the small box located in his car.

Chick Lancaster said, "Why would they be coming *here?*"

"It might be interesting to find out," offered Doc.

They had seen no trace of the car, and yet, by following the signals emanating from the device which the bronze man had placed in the trunk of the other car, they had been able to keep the other machine within reach. From the intensity of the signals, Doc Savage judged that the other machine was not more than a mile ahead of them.

They passed through city traffic, came to a wide boulevard that led into the heart of the city. Far down its length was the golden, shining dome of the capitol building.

The girl's eyes widened. "Do you think," she asked, "they would be going there?"

Doc's eyes were thoughtful. "We'll see."

For a moment, the signals faded. Then they picked them up again. The bronze man frowned slightly. At the next intersection, he swung right, proceeded for three squares. The signals were stronger again. Doc turned left on a through highway that passed out of the city.

"I guess those men aren't stopping here after all," the girl said.

Doc drove in silence. Shortly they were passing an exclusive section of large estates. Houses became more scattered. What few there were appeared only briefly through the trees of broad, sweeping lawns.

The road curved. High stone walls replaced hedges and lawns. It was impossible to see the homes now.

The signals suddenly became very strong in their ears. Doc's unusual flake-gold eyes were sharp. When the signals suddenly started to fade again, he slowed the car and turned around in the roadway.

The girl looked at Doc.

"What is it?" she wanted to know.

"We have passed the other car."

"But there was no side road, no place where they could have turned off!" the girl exclaimed.

Doc was proceeding slowly along the road. Directly before the entranceway of a huge estate, the signals became strongest, Doc noted the name of the estate as he swung the car into the graveled drive that wound beneath old elms.

Chick Lancaster suddenly gave a start.

"Do you know what place this *is?*" she exclaimed.

Doc nodded.

"The home of Governor Bullock," said the bronze man quietly.

"But—"

Doc held up his hand, indicated the huge house of block stone ahead. The gravel drive swung beneath a porte-cochere of the house. The signals were still plain in Doc's car.

But there was no sign of a machine parked before the governor's mansion.

Doc drew up, stepped out of the car and mounted the steps. There was a screen door; beyond this a door which stood open. The man lying on the hall floor behind the screen door was moaning and trying to get to his feet.

Doc Savage flung the door open, hurried into the hall, was quickly helping the heavy man to his feet. The costume of the man showed that he was a butler.

There was a nasty red welt on the butler's forehead. For a moment he stared dazedly at the bronze giant. Then his gaze sharpened and he exclaimed:

"You're Doc Savage! You're the man Mr. Bullock was expecting!"

Doc said, "What has happened?"

The butler was trembling. "Some men, some ugly fellows, were here just a few moments ago. They struck me when I told them Mr. Bullock was missing since last night. They wouldn't believe me!"

Doc's eyes flashed. "Missing? How do you know?"

"Mr. Bullock left here for an important conference at his executive office last night. He has not been seen since!"

"And the men that were here a few moments ago?"

"Gone!"

Doc swung toward the doorway. "You'd better bathe that head," he said, and started out.

"Wait!" the butler called, and he was suddenly handing a long white envelope to the bronze man. "Mr. Bullock left this last night, saying to give it to you if you called while he was out."

Doc started to open the envelope, remembered the signals that they had still heard as they drove into the estate. There was still the trail of the five men to follow.

He put the envelope in an inner pocket, hurried back to the car and got the machine started. He followed the drive that circled the mansion and cut down through a wooded lane beyond the estate.

The signals were abruptly very loud again.

Chick Lancaster cried, "They must be very close!"

Doc rolled to a stop a dozen feet before a rustic wooden bridge. The bridge formed part of the roadway, and spanned a brook that was part of the estate.

The girl was suddenly out of the car beside Doc Savage. Through the open side window of the bronze man's car, the transmitter signals were very loud.

Frowning, the girl said, "That's queer! How can the signals be so strong when their car is not even in sight!"

They were at the bridge. Suddenly Doc's gaze veered off to the side. In the next split second he had shouted the warning.

"Look out!"

With blurred speed, Doc swung the girl's trim figure into his arms and leaped backward.

The bridge before them went up into the air in a shuddering, earth-rocking blast.

Chapter X

THE BIG PEOPLE

The house was one story high, badly in need of paint, and looked like something ordered from a mail-order catalogue. The name on the tin mailbox outside the gate said:

ZEKE BROWN

Reds Lancaster, engineer, pointed at the house and said, "This is where he lived. Alone. He must have learned something, and because of that he died."

Monk and Ham had stepped out of the engineer's car. Learning that both were interested in all movements the farmer, Zeke Brown, had made before his mysterious death, the girl's engineer brother had obligingly offered to show Monk and Ham where the man had lived.

It was four o'clock in the afternoon, and the day was hot. The two pets, Habeas and the runt ape, had climbed out of the car and were lying down in the grass, to cool off.

Monk, frowning, muttered, "Blast it! I'd like to know what Zeke Brown had in that package for Doc."

Reds Lancaster was swinging his car around in the roadway. He leaned out and said, "There's a new shift going to work at the shaft at five. I'll have to get back. I'm putting Hardrock Hennesey in charge as walker."

Ham ignored some remark that Monk was making, looked at the engineer and asked, "Walker?"

"Superintendent in the tunnel," Lancaster explained. Sweat stood out on his freckled face. The collar of his flannel shirt was open and his necktie pulled down, a wet, tight knot over his chest.

He added: "If I can be of any help, let me know."

He left them there and headed back toward Shaft 9.

Monk had started toward the house. Habeas got up out of the grass and ran after him.

Ham and the pet chimp followed. The lawyer was saying, "I don't see where you expect to learn anything here, dunce?"

Monk had found the kitchen door open, was pushing inside the house.

"Listen," Monk rapped, swinging on his partner, "we've checked on all Zeke Brown's movements on the day he died, haven't we?"

Ham frowned. "I hate to agree with you, ape, but the answer is yes."

"And we learned, as far as everyone knows, that he didn't leave his home all day?"

Ham nodded.

"And yet," continued Monk, "Zeke Brown had a package which he was gonna mail to Doc. He went out last night to mail it. And half an hour after he left this house he was dead. Maybe we can find some blasted thing here that will show us what he was gonna mail."

Ham shrugged. He started to say, "I might as well humor you. Otherwise—"

He paused, listening. Monk, too, was peering curiously toward a hallway that divided the house. They were standing in the kitchen, and the sound came from across the hall, from what was apparently a bedroom.

It was a creaking; steady, frequent.

Monk suddenly swung toward the hall. Ham held his sword cane in a ready grip as he followed.

In the doorway of the other room, hairy Monk drew up short, craned his short neck, exclaimed, "Well, I'll be a ring-tailed baboon!"

The old fellow sitting in the creaky chair, rocking, must have been all of ninety years old. He had skin like leather that has been in a fire.

He looked up at the homely chemist and said, "Have you seen them?"

"Seen what?" Monk demanded.

"The people?"

"What people?"

"The people that lived here in the ground. The big people looking like giants."

Monk gulped. "What the blazes!" he piped shrilly.

The old fellow kept on rocking in the creaky chair.

Hairy Monk stood staring at the old fellow in the chair.

Ham did likewise.

The two pets, the pig and Chemistry, stuck their heads between Monk's bowed legs and looked also.

"Crackpot!" was Monk's comment, looking at his partner.

"Crazy as a bedbug," agreed Ham.

For the moment, they forgot that they were mad at each other.

The old brown-looking fellow stopped his rocking, glared at the two and said, "Maybe you'd like to see one?"

"See what?"

"One of the big people."

Monk looked at Ham, grinned, whispered, "We'll humor him."

They stood aside while the bent old fellow got out of the chair, led the way through the kitchen and out of the house. He followed a path that led to the old barn. The barn, which had once been red, looked so decrepit that it was about ready to lay down on its side.

The old man went inside. The place was shadowy, smelled of old hay. Somewhere a bee buzzed listlessly in the heat of late afternoon.

The old man proceeded to a pile of straw in the back of the barn and started shoving some of it to one side. Suddenly the pig, Habeas, let out a snort and backed away. Chemistry scrambled up a nearby ladder.

Monk said shrilly, "Blazes!"

The skeleton was about eight feet long. The size and shape of the bone structure indicated that the skeleton's original owner must have been a person at least nine feet tall.

The skeleton had been carefully concealed by the straw.

"You see?" the old fellow said.

Monk stared. "Whew!" he whistled. "I'm glad that guy ain't *alive!*"

Ham was bending down, examining the skeleton.

"I can show you another one," abruptly put in the old man.

Monk was interested. He was thinking of the thing they had seen down in the tunnel—evidence that, centuries ago, there had been another form of life in this locality. A coastal region that had been fifteen hundred feet below where they stood now.

"Where's this other one?" he prodded.

"'You come with me," the withered old man suggested.

Ham was still bending over the skeleton. He looked up at Monk. "I thought we were going to look over the house," he said. "You wanted to find out about that package Zeke Brown was going to mail to Doc."

"I'll be back," Monk said. "First, I'm gonna find out what else this old geezer has found."

Monk followed the old fellow out of the barn and across a field. They reached a wooded area beyond, and the old man kept on going, following a trail that led deeper and deeper into the woods. It was cooler in here, and the sun was kept out by the heavy top growth of the trees, which made the place look as though the sun had gone down.

Later, the sun had gone down and the old fellow was still walking, setting a good pace for one so old.

Monk complained, "Hey, grandpop! When are we gonna reach this other guy?"

"Soon now," the old man said, and he kept plodding ahead.

It grew darker. Silence lay like a heavy blanket over the wild section. Monk was about ready to say the hell with it, and return, when the old man paused and pointed ahead.

"This is the place," he said.

It was a small clearing. Evening dusk made everything shadowy and vague. The old man pointed to a pile of carefully placed rocks that looked not unlike an altar. On this rested the indistinct, long form.

Monk stalked across the clearing and bent down to examine this second skeleton, and the thing got up and took hold of the hairy chemist's neck.

It occurred to Monk, in the next wild moment, that what had hold of him was no skeleton. It was a human figure, about the biggest the chemist had ever tackled, and the fight that followed was terrific.

The big man bounced the chemist on the skull with something that felt like a large, round rock. But it proved to be a fist.

With a roar of rage—Monk always made bull roars when really mad—the chemist tore free of the fellow's powerful hold and started swinging his fists. He slammed into his assailant and let go with smashing rights and lefts.

And the big man merely let the blows roll off his barrel chest and laughed. He laughed harshly and bounced another fist off Monk's head.

Monk sat down on his hind quarters. He leaped up again.

And was immediately knocked off his feet.

The chemist spun around, dived behind the rock pile and got two good-sized rocks in his fists. He let them fly. The big fellow got back in the shadows and ducked low, but Monk kept picking up the rocks and hurling them in the general direction of the fellow's indistinct form.

Somewhere back in the woods there sounded a cackling laugh. The old geezer!

Wild with rage at being tricked like this, Monk

let a couple of rocks fly toward the source of the sound.

A rock came back and hit him in the chest, knocking him flat. Monk crawled to his feet dizzily, stayed in a crouch behind the rock pile and was more careful from then on. Nevertheless, he kept up his barrage of hurtling rocks. He kept it up until his arms grew weary and he was forced to stop for breath.

And then, puzzled, he listened.

There was no sound in the dark clearing. No rocks were flying back at him. He was, apparently, alone.

He crept forward cautiously, hoping he might find an unconscious form. A moment later, Monk swore.

For all he found was a large rock pile across the clearing. He had practically moved the stone pile from one spot to another, in his wild barrage.

Monk stood there swearing for two minutes without repeating himself once.

And then the light hit his homely features and Ham's voice said:

"I always figured you were crazy. Now I know it!"

Habeas, the scrawny pig, raced across the clearing ahead of Ham. He leaped up into the chemist's arms and licked his face.

Ham said, "For once, you hairy mistake, that ungainly animal showed sense. He got worried right after you'd left and kept pestering me. So I followed."

Monk exclaimed about the fight.

"The guy musta been a mate to that one back in the barn!" he muttered.

"You mean—"

"Like a giant," Monk continued. He picked up two large, round stones and glared off into the woods. "Come on. We'll find them."

Ham said, "Wait! We've got to hurry back."

"Why?"

In the flashlight glow, Ham's face was suddenly worried.

He said, "Reds Lancaster called that farmhouse. Renny heard something from the State capitol and asked him to get us as soon as possible. Lancaster is going to meet us back there at the farm."

"What's the trouble?" Monk demanded.

Ham was already leading the way back through the woods. There was anxiety in his words as he went on, "I don't know what it is. But that girl's brother seemed mighty worried about something."

They set a fast pace, the two pets running along behind them. The moon was up by the time they returned to the dead farmer's house. They saw the red-headed engineer's car parked in the roadway in front of the place.

Lancaster hopped out at sight of them. His wiry, alert form was tense.

"We've got to hurry!" he said.

"It's something about Doc?" Ham prodded.

The engineer nodded, motioning them toward his car.

"Chick called from the capitol. It seems she and Doc Savage were almost blown up near a bridge on the governor's estate. She was knocked out by the blast."

"And so?"

"When she woke up, Doc Savage was missing."

Chapter XI

THIRD DEGREE

The hotel room was stifling hot, and for a good reason. All windows of the large room had been closed tight and the shades drawn. Outside in the night the thermometer registered eighty. Inside the stuffy room, with the lights turned on, it was well over ninety.

Pretty Chick Lancaster sat tied in the straight-back chair and perspiration dripped off her smooth, high forehead. Her auburn-red hair was moist against her forehead; little curls of it clung damply against her neck.

But her blue-green eyes were bright and blazing.

She glared at the circle of men grouped around her and snapped, "For the hundredth time, you can go to hell!"

"Little spitfire!" one of the men said wearily.

The fellow's shirt was open at the neck and his sleeves were rolled up. The shirt stuck like wet sheeting to his shoulders. He had a hard, cruel face.

The other four men with him were equally as hard-looking. They also appeared disgusted.

They all stared at Chick Lancaster, and one said, "Maybe she doesn't know where the bronze guy is. Maybe she's just givin' us a stall."

For several hours now, the questioning had been going on. The men took turns firing questions at the girl. They were pretty good at it.

They should be. At various times in their questionable careers they had all been in police line-ups and been given the third degree.

A bridge lamp had been tilted so that the bright light hit Chick Lancaster in the face. Her features were flushed from concentration of the light. A tiny vein in her smooth throat throbbed.

But her chin was held high and her gaze was fiery. She had steadily refused to answer any questions hurled at her by the five thugs.

One man snapped, "Dammit, we gotta find Doc Savage. That was the big boy's orders!"

"Maybe *you* can make her talk?" someone asked.

"Maybe I can," said the man in a quiet, flat voice.

Heads turned to look at him. The fellow had an ax-shaped jaw and there was something about his eyes that made you uneasy.

Chick Lancaster, hearing the tone of his voice, stiffened imperceptibly. She saw the man stare at his fingernails, then polish them on his shirt sleeve. He looked at his nails again and then up at the others.

"I got some pliers down in the car," he said significantly.

He held his fingers up to the light and looked at the nails again.

Chick Lancaster shuddered. She had heard of torture methods used by crooks. She had heard of pliers being used to pull out fingernails.

Horror took hold of her. She was terrified because she did not know what she would do if they tried such methods. *She did not know where Doc Savage was!*

For when the blast had demolished the small bridge on the governor's estate, she only remembered being swept up into the bronze giant's arms, as he made an attempt to pull her clear of the danger. And then the blast had knocked them both flat and she had recalled nothing more.

Nothing, that is, until she woke up in the sedan with these five thugs. And now, for hours, they had been questioning her about the bronze man's whereabouts. After dark, she had been carried, gagged, up a fire escape of this hotel. She had screamed once the moment they had taken the gag out of her mouth. And a man had laughed.

"Yell your head off, baby," someone had said. "No one in *this* place is gonna ask questions. They know better."

And now—

The hatchet-jawed man who had mentioned the pliers started toward one of the windows. It was one containing a fire escape outside. He turned back and said, "I left the car down back in the alley. I'll be right back."

His companions waited quietly, staring at the girl.

She felt suddenly faint, thinking of what was going to happen when the cruel-faced man returned. But she gritted her teeth and sat there with her hands clenched behind her back, where the wrists were tied tightly together.

"Better decide to talk, babe," one man said. Sweat made his face appear like pasty dough.

"Joey doesn't fool," put in another.

Joey was apparently the one who had gone down the fire escape. He had not bothered to close the window, merely pulling the shade down to the sill behind him.

It rustled slightly in a hot, languid puff of breeze that drifted in from the night. The men continued to sweat as they watched the girl. One swore.

The shade rustled again and a man looked up and started to complain, "What the hell kept—"

Various things then happened, none of them expected.

Standing just inside the window, Doc Savage, looking like a great bronze statue, said, "You should have kept Joey inside."

The four men dived for guns at the same instant the bronze giant dived for them. They would never be able to understand how Doc Savage moved a dozen feet while their hands were only moving inches.

Doc hit the group before the guns were clear of shoulder holsters. Furious action followed. Two men fell down. They didn't get up again.

A third tried to slug the bronze fellow. He never saw the fist that lifted him off his feet as it cracked beneath his jaw. He landed in a heap beside the first two.

The fourth man tried to dive for the hall door. Fingers seized his throat, and pressure touched a certain nerve. He went quietly to sleep.

Doc Savage turned his attention to the red-haired girl. Untying her, he said quietly, "You should have stayed at the shaft with your brother."

The girl stood up from the chair, moving her slender arms to restore circulation. She smiled fondly at Doc Savage, exclaimed, "I wouldn't have missed this for the world!"

The bronze man made no comment. His metallic features were expressionless. He had already turned to start tying up the four men with the cords that had been used on herself.

Chick Lancaster shrugged and gave a little sigh.

This bronze fellow was certainly different from most men. She couldn't figure him out.

She asked, "What happened back there by the bridge? All I remember is—"

"We were knocked down," Doc explained. "You were merely dazed for a few moments."

"But—"

"They must have needed something out of the trunk. That explains how they found the miniature short-wave radio transmitter. They put the transmitter a hundred yards down the bank of that brook and set the trap. They captured you while I was down there looking for the transmitter."

Chick Lancaster's blue-green eyes were wide.

"Trap? You mean, we were supposed to be killed there at the bridge?"

Doc nodded.

The girl stared at Doc Savage. "I'm beginning to understand the kind of dangerous life you lead," she said.

Doc had all four men tied up. He picked up one man, set him in an armchair, then took something that looked like a small hypodermic needle from a vest beneath his coat. The captive's shirt sleeve was already rolled up, so Doc Savage merely stuck the needle of the gadget into the man's arm and pressed a small plunger.

Watching, wondering what this was all about, Chick suddenly remembered something.

"Look!" she exclaimed. "I just thought. How did you happen to *find* me?"

Doc looked up at the girl. "The police were given the license number of their car two hours ago," he explained. "It was located in this neighborhood just a little while ago. A few minutes ago I caught Joey entering the car."

"And the police?"

"They were merely requested to let me know where it was last seen."

The girl stared. "Then you have connections with the police here?"

Doc merely said, "We have worked with the police of various large cities at different times."

He did not explain that he was an honorary member of the F. B. I. and the New York City police department; that in practically every city through the country, he would gladly be given a free hand to do what he chose.

The fellow who had been administered the drug was suddenly mumbling.

"What did you do to him?" Chick queried.

Doc stated several long words. "In short," he added, "truth serum. We will try to find out what he knows."

The man's eyes were open. At first, he looked at the bronze man sort of vaguely. Then his eyes widened and he said, "I'm supposed to kill you. You're Doc Savage."

"Why are you supposed to kill me?" Doc prodded.

"Because they are not sure just how much you know?"

"Who?"

"The rest of them—the guys I'm working with."

"And who's that?"

The man answered the questions readily enough.

"Oh, Joey and Louie Heller and the Kid. All of 'em."

Doc Savage frowned slightly. Names of ordinary hoods and gunmen were not what he was seeking. What he needed was the name of the big-shot, the person who might know about the strange mystery that had hit Shaft 9 and why it had done so.

He asked: "Who is behind you? Who is paying you?"

The captive shrugged. "We call him Lefty. That's all I know about him. But he's working for some one still bigger."

"Who?"

The man was obviously now trying to avoid answering the questions. He looked suddenly pale, frightened. But the words came out against his will.

"I heard Lefty say something about . . . about Governor Bullock."

Chick Lancaster gasped. "No! It *can't* be!"

Doc looked at their captive. "Governor Bullock?"
"Yes."

Doc questioned the fellow further, but learned nothing. The captive only knew what he had overheard Lefty say. Lefty had merely hinted that their pay was coming from the State capitol itself.

Doc gagged the man, as he did the others—they were showing signs of returning consciousness—then stepped to the phone located in the room.

He called police headquarters, identified himself, reported that there were four thugs tied up in the room and a fifth in a car down in the alleyway.

He hung up.

The girl was still stunned. "I can't *believe* that it is the governor," she said. "I happen to know him well. Why, he's—"

"It might be a good idea to see him," suggested Doc.

"But how? That butler told you he was missing. He—"

Doc reminded Chick Lancaster of the note that had been handed him at the governor's estate.

"It was a message saying to meet him at the Mountain Hotel," Doc explained. "Governor Bullock is hiding out there. His life has been threatened."

The girl gasped. "But if he *is* behind this mystery, why would he be in hiding?"

Doc said, "That is why it might be interesting to see him." He stepped toward the fire-escape window, motioned the girl to follow. It was obvious that Doc wanted to avoid detection as they left the hotel.

He paused before helping the girl ouside, and said, "But first there is something else. A phone call to the shaft revealed that you are in the custom of staying at the Plaza Hotel when on trips to this city. I called them, and the desk clerk said there is a package there for you."

"Package?"

"Yes. A package for me, but sent in your care."

"What could it be?"

Doc said, "We had better hurry."

Chapter XII

THE PHOTOGRAPH

The package was about six inches square and a half inch thick. Chick Lancaster handed it to Doc Savage with the comment, "What *can* it be?"

The bronze man was seated behind the wheel of his big car. He had waited, because he had not wanted to be observed, while the red-haired girl had gone into the hotel where she was in the habit of stopping while in the capital city.

Doc unwrapped the package while Chick Lancaster watched. Inside, two pieces of cardboard protected a photograph that was new and glossy. It was about the oddest-looking picture either had ever seen.

Chick exclaimed, "Heavens! What *is* it?"

Doc was gazing intently at the photograph. He said nothing for a moment.

It was a view that might have been taken in some sort of tomb. Weirdness best described it.

Rock walls formed a background for what was some kind of ancient chamber. Crude weapons leaned on the wall. On the rock floor, a skeleton lay in a grotesque position. Off to one side there was a huge thing that looked like great slabs of marble embedded with crude wood spikes.

The man was pressed between these body-piercing slabs. It was evident that he had died hideously.

But Doc Savage seemed more interested in the size of the skeleton shown lying on the rock floor. From his vest pocket he took a small rule. He measured the length of the picture and the size of various ancient objects shown in the torture room. In his mind, he calculated the size of the skeleton. He remarked:

81

"No person living today would be as tall as that."

The girl gasped. "What does it mean?" She was pointing at words printed across the bottom of the picture. They read:

MEN SHALL DIE WHEN THEY
DISTURB THE BIG PEOPLE

Doc Savage was holding the photograph at various angles beneath the dashboard light. There was something like a shadow across one corner of the picture. The shadow did not seem to be a part of the view that had been taken of the strange chamber.

The girl shuddered. "Heavens! What a horrible thing! Where do you imagine it was *taken?*"

"If we knew," the bronze man said quietly, "it might explain a lot of things."

He made no further comment. He locked the photograph up in a dashboard compartment of the car, put the car into speed and headed for the Morley Hotel, after asking Chick Lancaster which direction it was.

It was almost ten thirty when they stopped on a side street beside the tall structure where Doc Savage had mentioned the governor was in hiding.

Doc said, "Perhaps you had better wait here."

But the girl's eyes flashed. "Nothing *doing!* I'm going with you."

There was enough determination in her voice to show that time might be wasted in trying to dissuade her from going. Doc shrugged, and climbed out. He locked the car and they entered the hotel by a side entrance.

The bronze man headed directly for an elevator that was standing open on one side of the large lobby. The car, except for the operator, was deserted.

Doc said, "A friend is ill. Would you take us right up?"

The operator quickly closed the doors and Doc and the girl had the car to themselves.

But in the hallways of the fourteenth floor, she

looked at him and asked, puzzled, "How did you know—"

"Governor Bullock is registered here under the name of Samuel Jones," Doc explained. "He is in Room 1401."

Room 1401 was at the end of a long, carpeted hallway. Doc knocked quietly on the door, stood waiting.

After a while a voice asked cautiously, "Yes?"

Doc Savage looked at the girl. She nodded.

"That sounds like the governor, all right," she whispered.

The bronze man said, "This is Doc Savage."

The door immediately opened and they stepped inside.

And immediately men with guns stepped out from where they had been pressed against the walls and covered Doc Savage and the girl. One said harshly:

"We kinda thought you'd fall for that fake letter!"

Because the red-haired girl was so close beside him, Doc Savage hesitated a moment before whirling into action. In that instant, guns were jammed into his spine and at least half a dozen men had him covered.

Chick Lancaster was seized by two other men. She started to scream. Immediately a hand was slapped roughly over her mouth and she was swept off her feet. She was quickly carried through a foyer and into a larger, inside room of what appeared to be a suite.

Doc was urged inside also. Two of the men remained behind him, two on either side. They were taking no chances on this bronze fellow.

The girl was being tied up and gagged. Doc was treated in like manner. There were so many guns covering him that he had little chance of trying for a break. Besides, there was the girl to think of.

Someone went through the bronze man's pockets, found his car keys.

"This'll be good," the man said. "We'll use his

machine. No chance of being grabbed now in that hot car."

Apparently Doc and the girl were going to be transported to some other point.

While the other gunmen waited, two men left the apartment. One was only gone two moments. When he came back, he said:

"Well?"

"Everything's fixed. We've got that guy on the freight elevator well greased. We'll take them down that way. Jimmie's gonna have the bronze guy's car waitin' in the alleyway out back. Come on."

While one man remained in the hall as a lookout, Doc and the girl were carried out by the others, hurried to a large service elevator around an ell in the corridor, placed inside and taken to the ground floor.

A dimly lighted freight entrance was revealed when the car came to a stop. The two captives were removed to an areaway behind the hotel. It was here that Doc's big limousine was pulled up.

The girl and Doc were dumped in the rear of the car. Two men climbed into the seat; three others got into the driver's section. Those who did not get into the car grinned down at the bronze man where his great form was jammed in on the wide floor.

"Be seein' you, Savage—in hell!"

The driver spoke to one of the men who were remaining behind. "You know where to meet us?"

"Yeah. You better get going."

"O. K."

The car rolled off into the night. The windows had been closed, and it was stuffy inside the car. The girl, Chick, was crowded between the two big men on the back seat. Each man held a gun. They watched Doc Savage more closely than they did the girl.

Doc was flat on his face on the floor of the machine. His hands had been tied behind him. His ankles were tied also, and yanked backward and upward so that they were tied to the ropes encircling his wrists. A gag was in the bronze man's mouth.

The driver wheeled the big car carefully through

city streets. He took no chance on being stopped by a traffic cop. Ten minutes later they were beyond the street lights and rolling through open country. The windows of the machine were opened.

Someone said, "Whew! I was damned near roasted!" as a breeze came in the windows and took away the thick stuffiness inside the car.

Doc Savage, with his teeth, kept working at the floor mat that was just beneath his face. His movements, so as not to arouse suspicion, had to be slight. He worked for perhaps twenty minutes before he had the corner section of the mat rolled back beneath his perspiring face.

His teeth closed over the tiny hook located there and he pulled on it carefully.

It was about a half hour after this, as the car was passing through a particularly lonesome stretch of country, that the plane came down out of the air and circled them and started dropping the magnesium flares.

The flares were bright enough that everyone in the machine was quickly blinded. The driver yanked on the brake, howled, "Holy hell! I can't *see!*"

"Turn around, you sap!" someone yelled. "It's some kind of trap!"

The driver started to swing the machine around in the roadway. He let out a shout. Behind them, another flare must have been dropped—for the space back there was a blinding sheet of white.

The car was completely surrounded by the curtain of intense whiteness, so brilliant that it was impossible to keep the eyes open for more than a moment at a time.

Suddenly, beyond that sheet of whiteness, a plane motor sputtered and died. Almost immediately there was a shout and a racket like a bull-fiddle roar.

The car driver slammed open the door and cried, "Me, I'm gettin' the hell outta here!"

That seemed to be the general idea of his partners. All piled out and ran like confused blind men through the white, burning magnesium glare.

There was the sharp crack of pistols. Over this, more of the bull-fiddle roaring sounds. And then, quite distinct, a voice that howled:

"Yeo-o-ow! I got me a blasted polecat!"

Chapter XIII

GOVERNOR MISSING

It was hairy Monk Mayfair who had yelled. Running from the plane toward the blinding white light, one of Doc's machine pistols in his hand, he had crashed into someone, a fellow wiry, slender and quick-moving. The magnesium glare was too intense to make identification possible.

But Monk got his huge hand on the man's coat and started thumping away on the captive's head with the butt of the gun.

It was Ham's voice that yelled, "Wait! You've got the wrong person!"

Monk thought it was a huge joke. "I should have hit you harder," he squealed.

The arrival of two of the escaping thugs from the car momentarily stopped the argument.

Monk grabbed a man. Ham had his slender sword flashing. Everyone started fighting enthusiastically. Three minutes later the two thugs lay sprawled on the ground and the two aids were trying to locate Doc's car in the blinding white light.

Somewhere ahead, Renny's voice roared, "Here it is, Lancaster. Come on!"

Ham and Monk, though they were blinded, moved toward the sound across a rough field. The two pets, Habeas and Chemistry, ducked in and out between their legs, also blinded by the light.

The four men—Ham, Monk, Renny and the girl's engineer brother, Reds Lancaster—had been flying toward the State capital when they had picked up the peculiar signal from Doc Savage's car. They had been using the fast plane left in the gas-station field when they had arrived at Shaft 9.

The signal was a short-wave code transmission that had automatically gone on the air when Doc had pulled the tiny hook in the floor of the car. The hook had switched on a small transmitter concealed beneath the floorboards of the big machine, and was only one of the scientific gadgets that Doc Savage had built into the unusual automobile.

Trailing the steady source of code signals, Renny —who had been at the controls of the plane—had located the bronze man's car speeding along the stretch of lonely highway. He had dropped low, released the magnesium flares that had blinded the car driver and his associates.

There was the sound of voices from somewhere within the curtain of dazzling whiteness. Monk squinted his eyes as he ran through the rough field, trying to see. He saw Ham just ahead of him. And then, abruptly, he couldn't.

Monk yelled, "Hey! Where are you?"

A form raised up in front of him. Ham!

Monk exclaimed, "Blast it! Where am I going?"

Spluttering, the lawyer said, "Into the river . . . I've just come out!"

The words came too late for Monk to check his waddling, fast stride. He plunged off a two-foot-high embankment and sprawled into the water. The water was only waist-deep, apparently a shallow stream that cut through the fields.

Monk came up snorting with rage. He glared at Ham, wading toward the opposite bank.

"I'm gonna flatten you for not letting me know that water was there!" he muttered.

Ham ignored the remark. The brilliant glow was dimming somewhat now; ahead, he had seen the car parked in the roadway just beyond a low fence.

Monk followed. The pets, looking like scared, wet chickens, scrambled after him.

Ham and the hairy chemist reached the car about the same time as huge Renny. The brilliant flares had dimmed enough now so that all could see.

Doc Savage had just stepped out of the car. He was helping the girl, Chick Lancaster, out of the rear seat.

Chick Lancaster stared at Doc Savage, gasped, "You were not *really* helpless, then? Why, you just now untied yourself!"

Doc merely said, "It was possible that they might have led us to where Governor Bullock was either waiting for them—or a captive. When I saw they were not going to do this, I figured we ought to try to seize them."

Doc explained briefly to the girl about the signal transmitter located beneath the car.

"Renny," added Doc, "had orders to come to the capitol tonight if we had not returned. I took a chance on catching them somewhere en route."

The girl's green eyes were wide. "But how did you know we were headed back toward the shaft?"

Doc raised his hand briefly, indicated a small compass that was a part of his wrist watch. "It was quite obvious as to the direction we were going," he finished.

Big Renny had been staring around. He asked abruptly, "Where's Lancaster?"

"My brother was *with* you?" the girl asked.

Renny, his long face as gloomy-looking as ever, nodded.

"He's been helping us all he could," explained Renny. "He came along tonight because he was worried about you."

They all started a search in the vicinity of the car. And a few moments later, all returned and gave the same report.

Lancaster, obviously, was missing.

Monk remembered the two men that had been knocked out and left back in the field. He started to say something about going back to get them, then looked at red-haired Chick Lancaster. He grinned at his partner Ham.

"You'd better go, shyster," he piped. "There's something I gotta tell Chick." He smiled fondly at the girl.

For Monk had gotten over his first suspicions of the girl. If she was trying to help Doc Savage, she must be O. K., in his opinion.

He stepped toward her now and said, "I've been worried about you."

Chick Lancaster gave Monk a warm smile. Then her lovely eyes clouded. She gripped the chemist's burly arm.

"What *could* have happened to my brother?" she asked worriedly.

"Maybe he's chasin' some of those crooks," was Monk's theory. "He'll be all right. He looks like a guy who can take care of himself."

Doc Savage said quietly, "We had better make a more complete search. Monk can bring back the two men who were knocked out. Chick had better wait in the car."

Monk sighed as he looked hopefully at the girl. "See you later, babykins," he said, and motioned to Ham.

"Come on, shyster."

Ham, his custom-tailored clothes clinging to him wetly, looked as though he was going to cut his hairy partner's throat as soon as he got him in a dark spot.

Still arguing, they returned to the spot where they had left the two men in the field—and found no one.

Monk stared. "Them danged polecats musta been found by the other guys who escaped from Doc's car!" he muttered.

They searched the field. They climbed a stone wall that separated this field from another beyond, a smoother stretch of ground where the bronze man's plane had been brought down by Renny. They even went to the plane to make certain that everything was O. K. The two aids finally returned again to Doc's car. The bronze man and big Renny had returned also, and they too reported no success in locating Reds Lancaster.

The girl, they found, was asleep in the rear of the car. It had been hours since any of them had had any rest.

Doc Savage was thoughtful a moment. Then he said:

"There is an angle to this that is very peculiar."

Doc told them the mystery concerning the disappearance of Governor Bullock, of the things that had occurred in the capital city. As yet, he had made no comment about the queer photograph sent him in care of the girl.

Renny suddenly boomed, "Holy cow, Doc! If the governor is mixed up in this thing, why would he have called you in to investigate?"

"Smoke screen," Ham, the lawyer, put in quietly.

Ham explained. "He could have called in Doc in order to throw suspicion from himself."

The bronze man's features were thoughtful.

"There is something that all of you should know about," he said abruptly. "It changed the whole aspect of the mystery."

"What?" Renny wanted to know.

"Governor Bullock practically financed Yellow River Dam and most of the water-tunnel project used in conjunction with it. That would hardly make him out a crook now."

"Then how do you explain his disappearance?" asked Ham.

Monk had a word to say before Doc could answer.

"How do you explain anything in this blasted mystery?" he demanded. "The giant skeleton thing, that death fog, those guys changing into mummies!"

Doc looked at Renny. "Have there been any more accidents at the shaft?"

The big engineer shook his head. "Nothing happened today," he said. "Everybody's back on the job."

The bronze man had apparently reached a decision. He motioned them into the car. The pets were already in the front seat.

"There is an answer to this thing somewhere in the State capitol," Doc said. "All of you return to the shaft. Perhaps you will find a trail to Lancaster. And you might try to find out who mailed the photograph."

All three stared.

"You mean," asked Ham, "the package that was missing from the farmer's car?"

Doc nodded. "It was a photograph, taken recently and readdressed to me in care of Chick Lancaster."

The bronze man got the photo from the car, showed it to the three aids.

Monk jumped. "Blazes!" he squeaked. "That's the same kind of giant skeleton we saw back in the barn."

"Barn?" asked Doc.

Monk told about the old fellow who had tried to trick him. He described the skeleton hidden in Zeke Brown's barn.

But Doc Savage seemed more interested in Monk's description of the ageless-looking old man whom they had met at the farmhouse.

"Find him," Doc ordered. "Look for me back at the shaft some time before tonight."

Leaving them with the girl and the car, he disappeared toward the field where the plane had been set down. A few moments later all heard the motor roar as the fast craft took to the air, circled once, then headed off toward the capital city.

It would be daylight in another hour.

Monk remarked, "Goshamighty! I just thought of something! I just remembered we didn't see Hardrock Hennesey all day. Now I wonder what's happened to *him?*"

Chapter XIV

HARDROCK FINDS A CORPSE

There were two others who were intersted in finding tough little Hardrock Hennesey.

The two were working on the muck machine down in the tunnel below Shaft 9. Powerful fellows, they wore the work clothes and metal helmets of muckers. They had gone to work on the midnight shift that same day, when a call went out for additional labor to help rush the tunnel job to completion.

Around them now there was noise and sweating and swearing. Air drills yammered in the hands of miners up on the platform of the tunnel head not far beyond them. An hour ago the tunnel had been cleared while a blast had been set off. Now the miners and the muckers were back in the bore cleaning out the cracked rock and muck. It was mostly rock.

One of the two men leaned on his shovel and spoke to the other. He almost had to yell above the racket.

"You know what?" he shouted.

His partner—a close look at the two men's raw-red hands would show that they were not used to this kind of labor—leaned on his shovel also and said, "Well, what?"

"I think that little Hardrock Hennesey has learned something. I just heard from one of the nippers that Hardrock is up there in the north extension of the tunnel. An' there ain't no guys working up there to-night!"

The other big fellow looked worried.

"Hell!" he exploded. "Maybe he'll find that—"

His partner nodded. "That's what I was thinking! We better investigate."

They dropped their shovels, approached a tunnel foreman and one man had a fit of coughing. He pressed his hands to his chest.

The other said to the foreman. "The dust has got him, boss. I'll have to take him up."

The first workman kept groaning and holding his hands pressed against his chest.

"All right," snapped the foreman. "Take him up."

Silicosis—a disease of the lungs caused by inhaling quartz dust—kills more tunnel workers than actual accidents. The foreman took it for granted that one of the two muckers had an attack of the disease now.

The two men hurried through the tunnel. After a while they were clear of the work gangs. They proceeded swiftly until they had reached the beginning of the long north extension from Shaft 9.

Here, work was practically completed. The report was that, tomorrow, the northern end of the bore would be blasted through to meet the tunnel from Shaft 10. And Shaft 10 was the last unit connecting with Yellow River Dam, the huge supply unit in the great project.

A nipper had just alighted from the bucket, having come down from aboveground. The "nippers" were the apprentices who kept the miners supplied with drills. They handled steel.

One of the two big muckers asked, "You seen Hardrock Hennesey, kid?"

The nipper waved a hand toward the north bore. "He's up there. He went in just as I was going out, about twenty minutes ago."

The two murmured something and hurried on.

They covered the four miles to the tunnel head. They passed no one. When they had gone as far as they could, one looked at the other and stared.

"Hardrock isn't here!" he exclaimed.

His partner, for a big man, looked scared. "That means," he stammered, "that . . . maybe he's found it!"

"Come on!" rapped the other, and they started running back through the tunnel bore.

Halfway to the base of the fifteen-hundred-foot

shaft entrance, they slammed into Hardrock Hennesey.

Hardrock eyed the two and said, his jaw thrust out, "I've been looking for you two buzzards."

There was a fight.

Hardrock Hennesey, as a kid, had been raised on the sidewalks of New York, in a section near Tenth Avenue. More than once bigger kids had beat him up, for Hardrock Hennesey had always been a pretty small guy.

And so he had learned, as he grew up, that there are other things to use besides fists. Because most men were usually bigger than himself, he generally went prepared.

What he used now was a pipe wrench yanked from the pocket of his too-big overalls. He sailed into the two big fellows like a Spitz dog going after two overgrown mongrels.

The wrench flew, and the two thugs let out assorted yells and Hardrock Hennesey got himself worked up to some nice plain and fancy swearing.

One man was slammed up against a hard rock wall of the tunnel. The other got hold of Hardrock Hennesey's arm and tried to twist it so that it would break and the wrench would be knocked free.

But the little tunnel worker sank his teeth into the big fellow's wrist. Howling with rage, the man sprang clear. Hardrock hit him with the wrench. He fell down, moaning.

The other one had come running back into the battle with his fists flailing and his head pulled down like a wrestler's. Hardrock tapped the man on the head with the heavy wrench, stepped aside as the fellow fell atop his inert companion.

Hardrock Hennesey spat out tobacco juice, put the wrench back in his pocket and said for the benefit of the surrounding grim walls, "About time I got those Doc Savage guys, I reckon."

When the sun was well up in the sky later that morning, Hardrock Hennesey located Monk, Ham and the big fellow named Renny asleep in the limousine of the bronze man. The car had been run beneath some willows at some distance from Shaft 9. It was a good shady spot where the sun would not bother them when it started to get hot.

Hardrock woke everyone up and announced, "I got something to show you."

Monk climbed out of the car looking disgusted and sleepy. Ham and Renny followed.

Renny asked, "What is it?" in his blasting voice.

"It's about that farmer, that Zeke Brown, who turned into a mummy. I know what he had found out."

"What?"

"You won't believe it unless I show you," said Hardrock Hennesey. "But I got wise to it when I followed an old buzzard that looks old enough to be Meth—what the hell was his name?"

"Methuselah," supplied Ham.

"Yeah—him," agreed Hardrock.

Monk was suddenly interested. He described the brown, leathery-faced old man who had tricked him at the farmhouse.

"That's the bird," said Hardrock. "Well, come on, and I'll show you something."

Hardrock suggested that they drive, and they all piled into the car. The pets, Habeas and the runt ape, were asleep on the floor in the rear.

Hardrock Hennesey gave directions, then looked worried and asked, "Where's Chick Lancaster? She all right?"

"We made her go home and get some rest," said Ham.

Chick and her brother, Reds Lancaster, lived in a rented house about a mile away from Shaft 9.

The route Hardrock Hennesey pointed out led away from the construction center, followed a dusty country road that ended in a meadow some distance behind the farm of Zeke Brown, deceased.

They got out and Hardrock led the way across a pasture. Habeas, the pig, immediately chased Chemistry across the field.

Summer heat had dried up the ground until it was like a baked, hard mud. They walked for some time, came to a hollow that dipped down beneath some trees.

Hardrock Hennesey indicated some dried-up tracks in the hard earth. "Zeke Brown musta been looking for a strayed cow," he said. "There's the prints."

"So what?" Monk demanded in his squeaky voice.

The little tunnel worker gave the chemist a cool look, led the way farther into the hollow. It became a crevice between ridges of land. Well into the opening, Hardrock suddenly paused and pointed at something hardly a dozen feet away from where they stood.

"What do you think of that?" he asked.

All stared.

The opening was a three-foot-wide crack in the earth. Cautiously, they moved forward and stared over its edge. The bottom of the thing was approximately twenty-five feet below them.

Big Renny studied the split in the ground a moment and then commented, "Some earth vibration has probably caused it."

"You ain't seen nothing," put in Hardrock Hennesey. "Wait a minute."

He moved off beneath the nearby trees, returned quickly with an armful of rope. He was paying out the rope as he returned, having, apparently, tied the other end to a tree trunk.

"Wait'll you see what's at the bottom of this place!" he exclaimed.

He caught hold of the rope, lowered himself over the edge of the crack, and slid downward. Shortly, the others followed.

In the bottom of the crevice, they all noted that it seemed to follow a well-defined fissure in the rock. Hardrock led the way.

It became darker and they appeared to be dropping lower at each step; and after a while the little tunnel worker took out a flashlight and indicated the way.

They had proceeded for perhaps twenty minutes.

They were below ground now, and it was cool and dank in the narrow passageway. Hardrock suddenly paused and said, "Here it is."

He pointed the light ahead.

Monk exploded, "I . . . ah . . . Jehoshaphat!"

The others merely stared.

The place had been widened into a sort of small room. And what was in the room was enough to create the horrors.

It looked like a medieval torture chamber. Crude, ungainly contraptions for tying up a person were built into the rock walls. There were sharp implements made out of quartz and stone.

On the floor there was a skeleton as long and as big as the one Monk had seen in the barn. A giant!

But the most awesome sight of all was the torture thing to one side of the roomlike space. Created of two crude slabs of granite, the machine held stone spikes that had been ground down to needle points.

A man was in the machine, and red liquid had oozed from his body and dried on the stone spikes.

Monk had a hard time getting out words. He blurted, "I . . . ah . . . Blazes! This is the same place shown in the photograph *that was sent to Doc!*"

Hardrock was staring intently at the dead man in the spike device. His intense gray eyes widened and he stared at his companions.

"Holy hell!" the tunnel worker gasped. "That . . . that guy in the machine! It's Jackhammer Edwards. A miner! He . . . he disappeared from the shaft a couple of days ago, I heard!"

Monk, curious, walked over and examined one of the hooks embedded in the rock wall. It, too, was of stone, as though made back in the dark ages.

Tugging at the hook, he exclaimed, "That old fellow might not have been so cracked after all. He kept talkin' about the big people."

The chemist turned and stared at the others. His homely face was puzzled. "Jeepers! What kind of people *did* live here in the earth?"

Monk had been holding to the stone-hook thing in the wall.

Suddenly Ham looked past Monk and yelled.

"Look!" the well-dressed lawyer rapped.

A foggy, vaporous spray was coming from tiny openings in the stone ceiling of the room. It spread, lowered swiftly, becoming like a grayish mirage. The room, within seconds, grew terrifically hot.

Monk let out a yell and leaped toward the others. "The fog!" he howled.

He started toward the opening where they had entered the room. And staggered backward as though he had been slammed with a massive fist. His homely features were blistered and his huge hands burned.

"We're trapped!" squalled Monk.

The opaque fog was fast growing more dense in the room.

Chapter XV

TUNNEL OF DOOM!

Late that same afternoon, every newspaper in the State was carrying black headlines. Word about the mystery centered around Shaft 9 and Yellow River Dam had leaked out. Also other facts.

A capital afternoon sheet ran the following:

GOVERNOR MISSING

Mystery Surrounds Tunnel Project as
Strange Fog Causes Deaths
and Terror

Capital City, August 3rd.—Though various State officials deny the fact, it has been learned on good authority that work on the ten-million-dollar Yellow River Dam and tunnel project has been stopped. A series of queer accidents have occurred on the construction job. Workmen, it has been stated, speak of a weird fog that appears and which turns men into mummies. Others even speak of a queer race of people that have been unearthed, and now men are too terrified to enter the various shafts.

This newspaper recalls a warning given months ago when Governor Bullock first broke ground for the mammoth Yellow River Dam. At that time, a committee of leading State businessmen and politicians held out for a site to be used in an adjacent valley to Yellow River. The site was considered more advantageous. But Governor Bullock, through a bond issue, had financed the site for the present dam and adjoining water-tunnel outlet. At the time, as many will recall, there was considerable argument over the entire thing.

And now, surprisingly, and as the mystery spreads at Yellow River Dam, it has been learned that Governor Bullock cannot be located. There have been hints of swindle. Has the people's money been invested in a project that is worthless? What has happened to Governor Bullock?

Doc Savage, a remarkable person who has solved baffling mysteries the world over, is reported to be at Yellow River Dam investigating. At this writing, Doc Savage could not be reached.

There was more, and at the very end of the newspaper story there appeared a box announcement set in boldface type.

BULLETIN

Three Doc Savage assistants are reported missing in tunnel mystery. The three men, accompanying a tunnel worker named Hardrock Hennesey, apparently were seen last at an early hour today. No trace has been found of them since. More details will be given here as soon as they are received.

Oddly, Doc Savage himself was in one of the very newspaper offices from which the foregoing information was released. It was the bronze man himself who asked that the articles be toned down. All facts concerning the tunnel mystery were not given to the public.

Two of the officials of the paper were on the committee that opposed Governor Bullock and his Yellow River Dam project. Doc had talked to them, and the others. One man in particular, a Colonel Henry Bishop, was returning to Yellow River with Doc Savage tonight. It was he who insisted that Governor Bullock was a crook.

While Colonel Bishop awaited Doc Savage in the executive offices of the paper, the bronze man went to the dark room of the newspaper and made a request. He would like to have use of their largest photographic projection equipment.

The request was quickly granted. Alone in the room, Doc Savage did a peculiar thing. Using special apparatus, he projected the photograph of the torture chamber onto a huge silver screen. He magnified the picture until it was "blown up" to a hundred times its regular size.

For a long time, Doc studied the projection. He seemed particularly interested in a shadow that was cast on one side of the picture. Just before Doc switched off the projector, his unusual trilling sound filled the quiet room. Apparently he had made some discovery which interested him.

Some time later, accompanied by Colonel Bishop, Doc Savage was returning in his plane to Shaft 9.

Colonel Bishop, politician and part owner of the *Sentinel*, was a man in his late forties. He looked like an unassuming clergyman rather than an aggressive State leader and a person reputed to be worth a million dollars.

He wore somber black and a flowing black tie. He had pale, almost scared-looking eyes that stared widely out from behind thick-lensed eyeglasses.

When Doc Savage brought his fast plane down swiftly for a landing in a field near Shaft 9, thin Colonel Bishop clung to the sides of his seat and looked as though he was going to be sick. This giant bronze fellow's dynamic personality sort of frightened him.

They had no sooner landed, and climbed out,

than a man whom Doc Savage had been seeking met them.

Reds Lancaster, the girl's engineer brother!

Doc inquired, "What happened to you last night?"

Lancaster was tense and excited. Apparently he knew the newspaper publisher, for he spoke to the man briefly. Then he turned his attention to the bronze man.

"I trailed two of the crooks almost all night," the wiry-looking engineer exclaimed. "I've found something!"

"What?" asked Doc.

"Peculiar animallike tracks, down in the north bore of Shaft 9. There's something damned queer we've hit down there. No wonder most of the workmen are terrified!"

"We'll investigate," Doc Savage said.

At the shaft, they met the girl, Chick Lancaster. The lovely red-haired sister of Reds Lancaster looked tired and pale.

She spoke to the bronze man about Monk and the others.

"We've searched everywhere for them!" Chick gasped. "And we can't find a trace of where they went. Hardrock Hennesey was with your three assistants—Monk, Renny and the one who is so nice—Ham."

Naturally the bronze man did not know about the four men being trapped by the weird fog. He said, "They are perhaps trailing something. All are capable of handling themselves."

But the mystery of their disappearance had even affected the tunnel workers. Hundreds of men milled about near Shaft 9, their faces grim in the glare of the floodlights at the shaft opening.

Only a few had been persuaded to stick to their jobs. As Reds Lancaster explained bitterly:

"We're blasting through the north end of No. 9 tonight. No. 10 is completed and hooked into Yellow River Dam. We're going to make a test."

"Test?" Doc prodded.

"Water is going to be released through the system," explained the alert, red-headed engineer. "We blasted through the southern end of No. 9 this afternoon. We're rushing things in an attempt to prove that the project is O. K., and before the rest of the muckers quit. We've *got* to!"

Chick Lancaster looked suddenly horrified. "You can't blast tonight!" she cried. "Perhaps those men—the ones with Hardrock—are down there some place!"

Reds Lancaster moved to his pretty sister's side, squeezed her slender arm. "Nonsense, sis. The tunnel has been searched from end to end. Besides, we can't wait any longer."

Colonel Bishop, his pale eyes wide, had been standing saying nothing.

He abruptly blurted, "I think I'll go up to your house, Lancaster. This . . . this whole thing gives me the horrors!"

He disappeared into the night.

Doc looked at the engineer. "But about these funny tracks you saw down there—" he started.

"Come on," suggested Lancaster. "I'll show them to you before we blast through."

A few moments later they were descending the fifteen-hundred-foot shaft in the bucket. The girl, Chick, had wanted to go with them, but her brother had argued her out of it.

Twenty minutes later, Doc Savage was being shown the peculiar tracks in the earth of the tunnel.

Several workmen had come down with them. The men carried powerful flashlights, battery affairs that sprayed light as bright as day over the tunnel walls.

The prints were like the tracks left by a man's bare feet—only twice as large. They appeared in some of the soft muck of the tunnel floor.

Lancaster asked, "What do you make of them?"

Oddly, Doc had not been examining the tracks closely. Unobserved, his interest seemed to be more intent on the walls of the water tunnel.

But now he looked at the tracks, turned to a

mucker and said, "You might give us a little more light here."

Behind Lancaster and the bronze man, who was bending down examining the earth, the workmen swung the light beams across the tunnel.

From where he crouched, none could observe the bronze man's gaze. It had flicked quickly to the tunnel wall beyond, was studying what appeared to be a large, grotesque shadow visible there. No one else observed the shadow, for Doc was careful not to lift his head too high. All thought he was studying the footprints on the floor.

But suddenly, the bronze man's trilling sound filled the bore. Musical, like distant winds stirring, it floated on the dank, close air.

A mucker gasped, "What was that?"

Others stared around.

No one had noticed the slight movement of the bronze man's lips as he made the unusual sound, an unconscious thing he did in moments of startling discovery.

Doc straightened up, said, "The tracks are very interesting, but obviously faked by the man responsible for this trouble here."

Muckers stared at Doc Savage. Reds Lancaster looked spellbound.

"You mean," he stammered, "there is . . . is something *explainable* about all this mystery?"

"Naturally," said Doc Savage quietly. "In fact, something has been made vividly clear to me."

Doc Savage would make no further explanations. It was his policy never to tell what he knew until he had a case completely solved.

But one thing was clear to those accompanying him now; Doc Savage, obviously, knew what the tunnel terror was all about.

Reds Lancaster was suddenly saying, "We'll have to hurry. We'll have to get out of here. The blast is scheduled for ten o'clock."

They had fifteen minutes in which to get aboveground!

Lancaster's auburn-haired, worried sister was waiting for them when they reached the surface. The bronze man drew the girl to one side.

He made a quiet request. He would like to know where there was a phone that could be used in private.

Chick Lancaster directed him to a community store that was located near the shaft. "There's a private booth in the back," she explained. "Old Milt is so deaf he wouldn't be able to hear you anyway."

Doc disappeared into the night. Oddly, he did not wait for the blast that was going to be set off in a moment or so.

In the store, within the private booth, the bronze man called a number in New York City. He talked several moments, then got the operator again and called another number. The bronze man made three calls in all.

When he came out of the store his metallic features were grimly thoughtful. He looked around for the girl, saw her running toward him.

Her face was white. She was trembling as she ran up to the bronze giant and cried frantically, "Reds —my brother—"

For a moment, it appeared as though she was going to faint.

Doc seized the girl's slender arms, demanded, "What's happened?"

The girl choked out stark words. "The blast . . . in No. 9 . . . they've set it off!"

"Yes?"

"And Reds . . . he's missing. *Someone saw him go down in the shaft just before the explosion!*"

At the shaft opening, there was yelling and confusion. Steel-helmeted miners and muckers were grouped around the shaft opening, staring out of horrified eyes at the bucket that had just been raised from the tunnel.

It was empty.

Doc Savage looked, said nothing. But he seized the girl's arm. "Come on," he said quietly. "From now on, you must stay with me. Your life is in grave danger."

The girl's eyes were wide with amazement. "*My* life? But what about my brother?

She drew back in horror as she realized Doc's purpose. The bronze man intended going below, into the tunnel.

"That explosion!" Chick Lancaster cried. "The water will be coming through. Oh, my God! Poor Reds—"

It was then that the bronze man made a strange statement.

"I don't think there will be any water," he said. "We will be able to enter the tunnel. Perhaps we will locate your brother."

Men protested as Doc and the girl climbed into the lowering device.

But Doc held up a bronze hand, said, "If we cannot get into the tunnel, we will signal you. The bucket can be then brought up again."

He motioned to the bellman, and then he and the girl dropped out of sight.

Someone said, "He's doomed!"

Chapter XVI

THE DEAD AND THE LIVING

They found the mummified man when they stepped out of the bucket at the base of Shaft 9. He was lying beneath a huge muck machine, his body mangled.

Chick Lancaster, showing the courage that was part of her makeup, rushed forward as some detail about the man's clothing riveted her attention. She bent down to look before the bronze man could stop her.

And then she had whirled away from the spot, terrible screams coming from her throat. She flung herself against Doc, beat at his great chest.

"It's Reds!" she sobbed wildly, and her slim body was suddenly quivering with choking sobs.

The man beneath the muck machine wore whipcords and a flannel shirt and high-top leather shoes. From a pocket of the whipcords was visible a length of watch chain; attached to this a small gold key with the name of a well-known engineering society. It was the key and chain that the girl's brother had always worn.

The rest of Reds Lancaster was unrecognizable. His hands, face, entire body—as Doc learned after a brief look—was a thing of dried-up, parchmentlike skin. Shriveled, as though by terrific heat that could have only come from one source.

The fog!

Doc examined the corpse's fingernails and skin ridges near the eyes.

Gently, Doc led the girl to one side. He went back and inspected the muck machine. A brief examination showed the bronze man that the machine had been tampered with, so that it would collapse the moment anyone turned on the power that operated it!

Abruptly, reaching their ears, there came a distant thumping, a sound as though someone was pounding on a solid wall of some kind.

Doc listened. He moved across to the girl and touched her arm. He said, "I realize how you feel. But I must ask you to come with me. You are not safe alone for a moment."

Chick Lancaster was too stunned to protest. She allowed the bronze man to lead her away from the gruesome sight of the crushed, mummified man. They headed northward through the great bore of the tunnel.

But even in her grief, Chick Lancaster's brain was clear enough to prompt a question.

"I don't understand," she said. "That explosion! That water that should be released from No. 10 bore! Why hasn't it been released?"

As they hurried through the tunnel, Doc, from time to time, had been glancing at his wrist watch. He drew up short now, held out his arm for the girl to see. Visible was the small, accurate compass which he had shown her once before.

"The tunnel should lead true north," he said.

She nodded, her eyes still misted.

"Look!"

She stared at the compass needle.

"But what—" she started to ask.

"Magnetic north!" Doc said. "The tunnel has not followed the original line plotted by the engineers. It tends to a slight curve west of north. There has been a mistake."

"Mistake?"

"They use a plumb line in the shafts composed of a heavy weight attached to a cable, which is lowered down the shaft, is that right?"

The girl nodded. "They use that to make certain the tunnel follows a straight line."

"Exactly," agreed Doc Savage. "But—that weight was magnetized by someone. It threw the calculations off. I examined one of the plumb-line devices yesterday."

Chick Lancaster was stunned by the information. She quickly understood why no water had been released into this tunnel from No. 10 by the explosion of the tunnel head.

"The two tunnels do not meet!" the girl cried.

Doc nodded.

They had been hurrying through the tunnel as they talked. The thumping sounds had become louder. Suddenly, they appeared to be right beside them.

Doc paused, swung around. One of the spring-generated flashlights was in his bronze hand, for the vague tunnel lights were too dim to reveal much of the rock walls.

Doc started to say, "It was just about here Monk cracked his head on what he thought was a—"

Then he stopped. The girl, too, stared.

It was as though the dynamite blast of such a

short while ago had found a weak spot in an earth fissure. For the rock wall had split. There seemed to be some sort of opening!

Doc plunged forward, the light in his hand. The girl followed. And before their intense gaze they both saw the heavy slab of rock that had swung aside as though it were a door of sorts.

Both peered past the opening.

"Good heavens!" cried the girl, her eyes wide.

Doc led the way past the crack in the wall. The place beyond was a huge, underground cavern. A great domed ceiling met their gaze. The vaulted passage stretched off to the right and left, and somewhere in the distance was the faint sound of water moving over stones.

And something else.

The thumping sound was loud now, as though someone were hammering on something.

The girl had started to move into the underground cavern. She turned back as she noted that Doc had paused, examining the wall through which they had entered.

Doc had taken out a penknife, was probing at the surface of the wall.

An exclamation escaped his grim lips.

"Glass!" he said.

"What—" the girl started.

"It is not a rock wall of the tunnel at all, but a glass section painted over to resemble rock. It is an opening through which anyone could have entered— or escaped from the tunnel."

Chick Lancaster stared. "But—"

Doc was bending down, picking up something that had been hidden behind the door. Moisture dripped from the domed ceiling over their heads as he moved, and ran down his corded neck.

The object the bronze man clutched was a cylinder, an aluminum-colored object about the shape and size of a small oxygen cylinder used in hospitals. There was a valve at the end of this thing, and Doc gave it a turn.

Immediately a vaporish, gray-white gas came from the nozzle. It touched the bronze man's hand, burned like hot fire into his flesh.

Doc jerked the valve closed, whirled the girl away from the spot. The odor of the escaping, foglike gas identified a chemical that he well knew.

"What is it?" Chick cried.

Doc waited until the small amount of escaped gas had dissipated. Then he moved carefully back to where it had struck the wall that was moist. The wall was absolutely dry!

And there was a livid, small burn on the bronze man's hand.

He said, "The formula is complicated, but briefly —it is a chemical that destroys water, breaks it down into its two components, oxygen and hydrogen. And in doing so, terrific heat is generated. Enough of that stuff would even dry the moisture out of a human's body."

Chick Lancaster gripped the bronze man's arm. She was trembling. "It . . . it explains the . . . the mummies!" she said.

Doc Savage nodded. The girl covered her face with her hands, thinking of the body they had just seen back by the muck machine.

The thumping sound from within the underground cavern had abruptly faded. Doc was straining his ears, listening.

He started to say, "We might—"

And then the yell came. A roar, rather, floating back from some distance. A voice that called:

"Holy cow! Monk! Ham! Look what's here!"

Doc and the girl raced through the great underground cavern. From time to time their feet struck loose sand. It was as though they were on the hard-packed beach of a section that had once been at sea level.

They ran toward the sound of Renny's voice.

Chapter XVII

DANGER OVERHEAD

The four men moved with weary steps. For hours they had been pushing their way through the vast underground caverns. For hours they had been without food. They had about given up hope.

Monk, his homely face gloomy, said, "You know what?"

The three men trailing behind him drew up short and looked at the hairy chemist's bedraggled appearance. The three men were Ham, big Renny and little hard-boiled Hardrock Hennesey. Even Ham's usually natty attire was soiled and torn.

Hardrock Hennesey spat, remembered that there was no tobacco in his mouth, swore and said, "Maybe we oughta go back to that torture-room place and try our luck at getting out the way we came in."

Monk jumped.

"Not *me!*" he piped shrilly. "We had a close-enough escape as it was. It was blasted lucky we found that way out of the room and into this cavern."

Renny nodded. "We'd better keep on the way we're going."

They were using a single flashlight. Above their heads moisture dripped from the great domelike ceiling of the underground passage. A dampness, a raw coldness, had got into each man's bones, and they were shivering.

Powerful Renny carried a heavy stone which he had picked up a couple hours ago. From time to time, he moved close to one of the rock walls and banged the stone against the surface. He had hoped to find some spot that might show a fissure by which they could get out. He had not been lucky.

The four kept walking.

Monk muttered, "I wonder if there really *are* some of them big people still living in this crazy world down here?"

Ham snapped, "Shut up. I'm trying not to think about it!"

Their steps lagged. Renny took the lead, being of more powerful build than the others. It was he who was carrying the light, and he got some distance ahead of them. They seemed to be climbing now, and the giant engineer's hopes had quickened. Thus he had forged on ahead.

And when his booming voice shouted back to them, all stood still for a moment in stunned silence.

"Holy cow! Monk! Ham! Look what's here!"

Monk, his bowed, short legs carrying him along furiously, for all his weariness, was first to reach Renny's side. The others arrived shortly behind him.

Renny was squeezed into a narrow crevice where there was barely room for his massive shoulders. His gloomy face turned back to look at the others. He yelled:

"There's something—here—ahead—that looks damned modern, or I miss my guess. Looks like a pipe!"

They all squeezed in behind Renny and urged him forward.

The round, huge thing gleamed in the light ray. They reached it. It was a pipe—a steel water-line pipe about eight feet in diameter. By the merest chance, Renny had spotted the thing at the end of the narrow defile leading out from the cavernous underground space.

They immediately started following the pipe line. At points it was necessary to crawl on hands and knees, to squeeze through knothole spaces.

They proceeded perhaps half a mile, and found that the pipe ended in a room that was apparently some sort of valve gate in the water system.

An iron ladder led upward. They scrambled up

the ladder, opened a huge steel cover. They were suddenly out in the night air.

For a while, it was difficult to get their bearings. But Renny, who knew more about engineering than the others, was first to figure out where they were.

"Holy cow!" he bellowed. "It's the dam. We're in some kind of sluiceway that runs off one side of the thing!"

High, concrete walls bordered them in on either side. The walls were higher than that found around any prison!

Ahead, a broad apron of concrete angled upward. Up, up! It stopped at a sheer cement wall that rose as high as the side walls themselves.

Behind them, the wide apron of concrete dropped downward in a spillway that ended at a drop-off a hundred feet above jagged, huge rocks.

All stared.

Monk voiced their thought. "How the blazes we gonna get outta this place?" he wanted to know, puzzled.

From far above their heads, the harsh, cold voice from atop the wall rapped: "That's just it. *You aren't!*"

They all craned their necks upward. The flashlight that Renny was holding outlined the wiry, alert figure of the man standing up there looking down at them.

It was the engineer brother of Chick—Reds Lancaster!

A moment later, another figure appeared beside that of the red-headed engineer. A man of about forty, wearing glasses and black clothes and a flowing black tie. He was extremely thin.

Hardrock said, "Who the hell is *that* guy?"

None could have known that it was the man who had accompanied Doc Savage from the State capitol —the newspaper publisher-millionaire, Colonel Bishop!

But all were certain of *one* thing. They had been tricked. The expression on the two men's leering faces above said that they planned death for these Doc Savage men and little Hardrock Hennesey.

Reds Lancaster had made a motion with his arm. A moment later there was a sound like a rushing of wind through swamp willows. What followed almost immediately held all four men momentarily frozen with horror.

Water. Tons and tons of water, suddenly appearing at the top of the spillway, hurtling down upon them.

Water that was being released from the storage lake that was Yellow River Dam!

Ham screamed a warning.

"Back inside. Hurry!"

They tumbled back into the opening that led into the valve-gate room. They slammed the heavy, round steel trapdoor over their heads. There was a heavy dog-arm arrangement that sealed the lidlike affair tightly in place.

Water was pouring through even as powerful Renny grabbed the levers and screwed the lid up tight.

Above them now, ominous in sound, water rushed past the slim steel protection and made the noise the sea makes against the side plates of an ocean liner.

At the bottom of the ladder, below them, Doc Savage said:

"It was lucky Renny called out your names while you were back in the cavern."

They looked down. They saw Doc and the girl, Chick Lancaster!

Monk, without thinking, started to yell: "Doc! Blazes! Guess who's behind this thing? He's up there on the wall and he's—"

Some expression in the bronze man's magnetic eyes stopped the hairy chemist from completing the statement. Doc was standing just a little in front of the girl.

He said, "The man's name is Colonel Bishop."

The girl gasped. "Bishop? The publisher? Why, good heavens, he's a friend of Reds'—" She remembered the accident at the muck machine. "He was a friend of my brother—"

She was suddenly in tears.

Doc Savage was listening to the sounds of the tons of water overhead. His metallic features were grim.

Ham yelled down, "We'll have to go back, try to find some way—"

But the bronze man was suddenly shaking his head.

"There is no way back," he pointed out. He indicated the girl. "We located a clever entrance from the tunnel into the underground caverns. Later, we went back to examine it again. It had been automatically sealed by some electrical device, apparently operated from aboveground."

Hardrock Hennesey stared at Monk. Ham looked at big Renny. And they all knew that as long as that spillway was open above their heads, they were trapped. They could be kept down here for days— weeks.

Doc Savage had suddenly motioned them down from the ladder. He had moved toward a heavy steel door on one side of the concrete-walled room. He turned back a moment and directed:

"You will all wait here. There's just once chance that the main sluiceway valve can be shut off—if the water in the dam is not too high to block off his passage."

He disappeared beyond the door, entering what was obviously a passageway beneath the great dam itself.

They waited. Ham, as gallant as ever for all his bedraggled appearance, held the girl's slim hand. He heard her story about the death of her brother, at the base of Shaft 9. He listened in silence and said nothing, but his eyes met those of his companions.

He, like Monk, Hardrock Hennesey and Renny, had seen Reds Lancaster a moment ago with their own eyes.

It must have been an hour later that they all stiffened, listening. The rush of water above them had slackened. It slowly dropped to a murmur. It finally stopped.

Renny yelled, "Doc's got it shut off!"

He piled back up the ladder, unloosened the heavy dog-arms, put his weight against the round trapdoor.

It lifted upward and water dribbled down his shoulders, and gloomy-looking face.

But the way out was clear.

A light beam hit their faces as they came out into the night air. Doc Savage's voice called down to them.

Grab the rope. Come up one at a time."

They tied the rope around the girl's slender waist first. They saw her pulled upward to safety. Renny, Ham and Hardrock Hennesey went up next.

When Doc dropped the rope down the last time, Monk didn't wait to be pulled up. He scrambled up the thing hand over hand like a happy monkey!

Atop the sluiceway wall, off to their left, they saw something in the dark night that held them momentarily rigid.

Two men, fighting, along the very edge of the great retaining wall of Yellow River Dam! While two hundred feet below, bellowing and waving their fists angrily, was a mob of tunnel workers from Shaft 9. The workmen held flashlights and flares. Obviously they were yelling at the two fighting men atop the great wall which towered over their heads.

But on top of the dam wall, the light was too vague to make identification of the two fighting men possible.

Monk was all for getting over there and investigating.

It was Doc who held him back. The bronze giant indicated the girl, whose face was still pale from the ordeal which she had been through.

He told Monk, "Take her up to the superintendent's house." Doc indicated the house overlooking the big dam, the home where Flynn, the superintendent, lived. "She has taken a slight chill," Doc said. "Hurry."

The assignment was one which hardly displeased the homely chemist. He lifted the girl into his arms and hurried off.

Doc swung back to the others.

"She must never know," he ordered.

Ham asked: "You mean, that her own brother, Reds Lancaster, was behind this mystery?"

The bronze man nodded. For one of the few times ever observed by anyone, slight lines of fatigue showed around his remarkable flake-gold eyes.

"Yes, that," said Doc. "Also, that he was merely a dupe for the *real* villain—Colonel Bishop."

Everyone stared.

As Doc Savage talked, his eyes were on the two men battling high up on the dam. He suddenly started in that direction, saying quickly, "We can figure out what to do with Lancaster *after* we rescue him. It appears that he and Bishop have split."

Renny, racing after Doc Savage, exclaimed, "That's *Bishop* up there fighting?"

Doc nodded, and as he swung up to grasp a ladder that led onto the wall, the others ran after him.

Chapter XVIII

DEATH FOR TWO

The distance to where the two men were struggling furiously near the sheer edge of the dam wall was perhaps two hundred yards. Doc and the others were almost to the spot when the bronze man drew up short, pushed the others back.

"Listen," he said warningly.

They all heard the shots. The gunshots that were accompanied by curses and loud yelling from below the wall, from the tunnel workers momentarily out of sight of Doc and the others.

The workmen, enraged, were shooting at the two fighting men—Lancaster and Colonel Bishop. The two crooks had been spotted, and now men were intent upon killing them!

Little Hardrock Hennesey wanted to get his hands on Reds Lancaster. He tried to get past the bronze man. Powerful Renny yanked him back.

Renny bellowed, "Fool! Do you want to get riddled with those bullets?"

They could hear lead smacking the wall of the dam, close beneath the feet of the two struggling figures. The slugs richocheted off the concrete, went screaming upward into the night.

For the moment, Doc and the others could do nothing. To move nearer to the fighting pair of men meant danger of being hit by a stray bullet. And so they stood tensely and watched.

A powerful spotlight being used by one of the workmen below the dam wall hit one of the struggling figures. It outlined the thin figure of the black-clad publisher—Bishop. The man's flowing black tie was in shreds; he was now without his glasses.

As they watched, Ham demanded, "But how is Bishop tied into this thing?"

Doc said, "Bishop owns practically all the property in the valley sponsored by the politicians opposing Governor Bullock. By throwing suspicion on the governor, and also creating a menace here so that the work would have to be stopped, he would force them to use the other site. Thus he would clean up a fortune when they came to buy the property."

"But Lancaster?" Ham prodded. "What about him?"

"Lancaster owes Bishop forty thousand dollars. Years ago Bishop helped him out of some sort of mess. Now he is forcing Lancaster to pay off. The girl informed me tonight that her life has recently been threatened. That was Bishop's trick to force Lancaster to do his bidding."

As he talked, Doc had moved closer to the two. So intent were they upon slaughtering one another, that neither had noticed the approach of the bronze man and his partners.

But more bullets arrived over the top of the dam wall. They whined past the ears of everyone. Doc and the others were forced to crouch low.

Lancaster and Bishop were rolling around in a tangled heap now, dangerously near the edge of the wall. Miraculously, the bullets missed them.

As they all watched tensely, Doc added another bit of explanation. "A phone call to New York revealed that Bishop was the owner of most of the property they would be forced to use. Of course, he was working through a false name, under a fake company."

Suddenly, before their eyes, a peculiar thing happened.

Colonel Bishop, with a frightful yell, swayed to his feet, clutching his thin chest. In his right hand was a gun. His own, apparently.

Obviously he had tried to use the gun on Lancaster. But the quick-moving engineer had managed to twist the weapon away from him. Bishop had shot himself.

He swayed. Even Lancaster looked amazed that such a thing could have happened. Perhaps he had not meant to kill Bishop. At least the expression in his wide eyes now said that he was startled. Unmindful of the shouts from below, he watched the wounded man.

And then, without warning, Bishop threw his toppling body against the engineer. In his last weak step forward, he knocked into Reds Lancaster.

Lancaster made a frantic attempt to catch his balance. His hands pumped the air as though he was making a frantic attempt to grab something. In the next instant he went backward over the wall and disappeared from sight. A scream floated above the yelling from below.

Bishop crashed into a broken heap at the very edge of the wall.

Doc and the others leaped forward. Disregarding the moaning man at their feet, they stared down the sheer length of the wall. They were in time to see

Lancaster's tumbling body strike the outward curve of the dam, two hundred feet below. It struck, bounced, then slid like a limp rag doll along the remaining seventy-five feet of dam footing. A wide swath of red fluid, revealed by the spotlights, was left behind the body.

Every bone in Lancaster's body must have been broken by the plunge.

Monk had arrived back from the superintendent's house in time to witness the death plunge of Lancaster. He stared now in awe.

Puzzled, he asked, "Doc, while we were waiting for you to shut off that water, the girl told us her brother died back there in the tunnel. She even said—"

"The person she saw," said Doc, "was the old fellow who tried to lead you into a trap earlier. I estimated his age from the ridges in his fingernails and from the crow's feet around his eyes. Lancaster saw that he was almost trapped. He was going to vanish from the picture. And so he made it appear that he had died. What he did was kill off that old fellow who had been working for him throughout."

Mention of the withered old man made Monk remember the giant skeletons and the horror chamber. He asked about that. Renny and Ham were bending down over the dying man.

Doc Savage said, "When the girl was with me in the underground caverns, she happened to mention the old Indian mounds that used to be near here. They unearthed some of the stuff when they first excavated. The Mound Builders left weird collections. Lancaster used the stuff to make it appear some race of people were still living there in the earth. In fact, there was an old museum near here once. It is now closed. Investigation will probably disclose that things have been stolen from the place."

Bishop, dying, had been propped up by powerful Renny. The man's dimming eyes sought the bronze man's. He muttered weakly:

"The photograph . . . I mailed . . . did not fool you!"

Doc shook his head. He said. "There was a shadow across one edge of the picture, Bishop. In your own newspaper building that photo was enlarged many times. Tonight, down in the tunnel, a workman's flashlight happened to cast an enlarged outline of Lancaster's profile on the tunnel wall. It matched, identically, the profile revealed by the enlarged shadow in the photograph. Lancaster took that picture, and inadvertently his own shadow was cast on a wall as he made it."

Monk suddenly remembered something. He made a dive toward the dying man. The chemist wasn't very particular whether the man was dying or not. Bishop was the real villain, and there was something he should know.

"Hey!" squalled Monk. "Betcha *he* knows about the governor!"

Doc pushed Monk back as he said. "Governor Bullock is safe at our New York headquarters."

Monk stared. "But how—" he started to demand.

Explaining another of the phone calls he had made tonight, Doc Savage said, "He went there because his life had been threatened." Doc told them about the letter handed him by the dazed butler at the Bullock estate. "The letter the governor *really* left explained that he was going to our headquarters. He had previously phoned and asked me to investigate this mystery. But his letter was switched for another by thugs who knocked out the butler."

The dying man gasped, "Has . . . *anyone* ever . . . outwitted you . . . Doc Savage?"

Monk started to blurt, "Brother, *nobody* fools Doc—" And then he paused.

Colonel Bishop was dead.

Later, following a circuitous route from the small valley below the dam, the tunnel men arrived at the spot where Doc and the others were grouped around the dead man.

One of the arriving men exclaimed, "Lancaster's dead. He tumbled off this wall—"

Doc Savage nodded. And then, holding up his hand, he made a brief speech. It was probably one of the most impressive speeches the bronze man ever made. He said:

"Lancaster, in a way, was a dupe for this man here." He indicated the dead newspaper publisher. Briefly he explained how Bishop was behind the mystery. He went on, "Lancaster is dead, but his sister believes he died down in the shaft. It is best that she always thinks that."

Doc mentioned the fight between the two men behind the mystery. "At the very last, Lancaster must have turned against Bishop. He had realized his mistake. And so now, and for all time, it is best that his sister know nothing of his connection with the real villain. Since he is dead, no good can be gained by making her suffer further."

There were shouts of "Bravo!" from the tunnel men. All liked Chick Lancaster. She was the kind of a girl who inspires admiration in brave men. All agreed to Doc Savage's suggestion.

Preparations were made for the removal of Lancaster's broken body, lying at the base of the great dam. Someone asked the bronze man:

"But what about that fog that turned guys into mummies?"

Doc told of finding the cylinders of chemical hidden in the cavern. He explained how the chemical broke down water and at the same time generated terrific heat.

"The heat," Doc pointed out, "was so intense that it literally baked a man's body. The chemical is also poisonous. Bishop planned on using it in the water system of the dam to make it worthless—in case his other plans fell through."

Tall, angular Flynn, the superintendent of the dam, arrived accompanied by the two pets, Habeas and the chimp.

Monk let out a joyous shout. Ham grabbed his pet.

The superintendent said, "They were just delivered to the house. They wandered back to the shaft tonight, half starved. But they had been fed."

Monk petted Habeas. Ham held the chimp in his arms.

The hairy chemist suddenly remembered the girl. He asked:

"How's Chick?"

"Got her wrapped up in bed with plenty of blankets," the superintendent said. "She's O. K. now. In fact, she's been asking for you two."

Monk beamed, and Ham looked pleased also. They led the way back to the house. In the lower hallway, they waited until the superintendent had gone upstairs to see if the girl was awake.

She was.

Monk's homely features split in a wide grin that threatened to dislodge his ears.

"Chick likes Habeas," he piped in his squeaky voice. "I'm gonna go upstairs and cheer her up!"

Ham pushed his burly partner aside. He gave Monk a frigid stare.

"She likes *me!*" Ham said icily. "Not that scrawny pig! Get out of my way!"

They both went up the stairs, arguing.